LOSING BASH

Charon MC

Book 9

KHLOE WREN

Books by Khloe Wren

Charon MC:
Inking Eagle
Fighting Mac
Chasing Taz
Claiming Tiny
Chasing Scout
Tripping Nitro
Scout's Legacy
Mac's Destiny
Losing Bash

Fire and Snow:
Guardian's Heart
Noble Guardian
Guardian's Shadow
Fierce Guardian
Necessary Alpha
Protective Instincts

Dragon Warriors:
Enchanting Eilagh
Binding Becky
Claiming Carina
Seducing Skye
Believing Binda

Jaguar Secrets:
Jaguar Secrets
FireStarter

Other Titles:
Fireworks
Tigers Are Forever
Bad Alpha Anthology
Scarred Perfection
Scandals: Zeck
Mirror Image Seduction
Deception
Mine To Bear

ISBN: 978-0-6486896-0-7

Cover Credits:
Model: Blake Savani
Photographer: Reggie Deanching of R+M Photography
Digital Artist: Khloe Wren
Editing Credits:
Editor: Carolyn Depew of Write Right

Acknowledgements

It's been a bittersweet experience to write Losing Bash. I've loved this man since he first appeared on the page and writing about his heartache definitely had an effect on me! And now it's time to hand him over into Janine's care. I'm sure she'll do him right and hook him up with his ideal woman.

I've never done anything like what Janine and I have done with this project and it's been an exciting roller coaster of a ride! I can't wait for you all to read Bash and Needles' journeys as they move across the country to get their fresh starts in life.

As always, a shout out to my husband and girls for putting up with me while I worked long hours to get this one written and published.

To my PA Andrea, who once more kept me sane and worked hard to help keep things rolling.

My street team, thank you for the support and encouragement.

To my betas Andrea and Miranda, I'd apologize for making you cry, but you know I wouldn't mean it! *wink*

xo
Khloe Wren

Biography

Khloe Wren grew up in the Adelaide Hills before her parents moved the family to country South Australia when she was a teen. A few years later, Khloe moved to Melbourne which was where she got her first taste of big city living.

After a few years living in the big city, she missed the fresh air and space of country living so returned to rural South Australia. Khloe currently lives in the Murraylands with her incredibly patient husband, two strong willed young daughters, and an ever growing list of animals.

As a child Khloe often had temporary tattoos all over her arms. When she got her first job at 19, she was at the local tattooist in the blink of an eye to get her first real tattoo. Khloe now has four, two taking up much of her back.

While Khloe doesn't ride a bike herself, she loves riding pillion behind her husband on the rare occasion they get to go out without their daughters.

Author Note

This story deals with a few medical conditions. My life has been touched by each of them.

My maternal grandmother suffered a brain tumor thanks to years of following her husband around as he raged and threw things in the air. She came out of the surgery with Parkinson's. I chose not to give Bash's mother this condition. Instead she suffers with early onset Alzheimer's. A condition my paternal grandfather suffered.

I personally suffer with PTSD and all that entails. The paranoia, anxicty, suicidal thoughts, depression. I've never turned to alcohol or been violent, but I know how common that is among sufferers.

As with any medical condition, each sufferer has different symptoms and coping mechanisms. The characters in this book are just a couple of examples and by no means cover the full spectrum of what people with these conditions suffer.

Charon:

Char·on \ˈsher-ən, ˈker-ən, -än\

In Greek mythology, the Charon is the ferryman who takes the dead across either the river Styx or Acheron, depending on whether the soul's destination is the Elysian Fields or Hades.

Prologue

November 2016
Scout

It wasn't every day a citizen was brave enough to approach me straight up. So as I sat in Marie's Cafe, sipping my coffee and keeping an eye on things, I took notice when an older woman I hadn't seen in over two years came in and paused to scan the room until her gaze locked on mine. With her head held high, she clutched her handbag strap and strode over to me. Woman hadn't changed a bit, not in all the years I'd known her. Laura Alfonsi was old school. She'd have to be in her late fifties, maybe early sixties now. Just as she'd always been, she was neatly dressed in a skirt and blouse, with her hair perfectly styled so she fucking looked like she'd stepped straight off the page of a 1950s housewives' magazine.

I had no fucking clue why she was looking for me. Her old man had passed away just over two years ago and I hadn't seen her since.

"Wonder what she wants?"

"No clue, brother."

Bulldog, my VP, was with me this morning, as he was most days.

"Mr. Dalton?"

Like I said, woman was old school and she'd always refused to use road names. "Yes, ma'am."

She stood a little straighter, as if she were surprised I would talk to her, or maybe she was steeling herself for whatever it was she came here to ask me for. Even when Frank had been alive, Laura hadn't spent much time around the club. She hadn't liked bikers as a rule and refused to get to know any of us so we could change her opinion. So many people figured bikers were nothing but trouble. Generally speaking, we were just like everyone else. We had our good and our bad, and sure, if you're fucking dumb enough to mess with us, look the fuck out, because we would come after you. But for the most part, we were more of the live-and-let-live mentality.

"I, ah, well, I was wondering if I could have a word with you?"

With a nod, I stood and held out a chair for her to sit. I figured she was here to ask me for something, and she was damn nervous about it, so it must be something big.

"Please, why don't you take a seat and tell me what I can do for you?"

"Ah, okay. Thank you." She lowered slowly into the seat and I returned to my place.

"Would you like a drink? Or something to eat?"

Again with the shocked blinking for a few moments. "Ah, an iced tea would be lovely, thank you."

Bulldog rose, and with a nod, headed up to arrange it for her. Once he'd left, she cleared her throat and folded her hands in front of her.

"I've come to ask a favor of you. My late husband, he told me if I was ever in trouble and he wasn't around, I should come to you. That you were a good man and would take care of me." She cleared her throat again and blinked back tears. I honestly had no clue where she was going with this but Frank hadn't been simply a club brother, we'd served in the USMC together, too. I'd only stayed in the USMC for four years, while Frank had been a career man. He'd come home in the end with PTSD and eventually it ate away at him until he couldn't go on. It was a damn shame, and it'd been hard as fuck to watch him around the clubhouse slowly lose himself to the demons in his mind that none of us could figure out how to save him from.

"Frank gave you good advice, Laura. I am the one you need to come see if you've got a problem. I will always be there for a family of one of my brothers, whether they're fallen or not. I am sorry we lost him, though. Waste of a good man."

She winced and waved off my final words. "He didn't come out of the corps as well as you." She trailed off and I winced at what she was implying. Not wanting to upset her further, I tried to get her back on topic as Bulldog returned and set a glass of iced tea in front of her.

"Oh, thank you so much."

I gave her a moment to take a mouthful, giving Bulldog a single shoulder shrug when he raised an eyebrow at me in question.

"So, what can I do to help you out?"

"My son, Jake. He's the only family I've got left. Not sure he realizes it yet, but I'm sick. It may be terminal, and I fear for how my boy is going to cope once I've gone."

I vaguely recalled Frank talking about his boy, but he hadn't been like some of the other club brothers, bringing him around to family barbecues on the regular. I saw him at Frank's funeral obviously, but that was over two years ago and I couldn't remember the boy's face clear enough to guess his age. "How old is he?"

"Twenty-three now. He's a construction laborer. He's a good boy and a hard worker, but he hasn't had the easiest life, not with his father coming and going, then when he finally returned for good, in the state he did. He's always been quiet and a bit of a loner and I worry for him."

At twenty-three years old, the man was a fucking adult. So I figured there must be more to her story. I sat forward, holding her gaze. "What, exactly, are you asking me for, Laura?"

"I'm asking if you'd take Jake under your wing. Maybe let him hang around with that club of yours. Give him the family he deserves but I never could give him."

This woman was breaking my fucking heart right now, and making me feel guilty as fuck for not checking in with her after Frank passed. Or even before he passed, for that matter. Frank had been a quiet man, apparently like his son, and as he got more paranoid, he grew even more reclusive. None of us realized how bad he'd become until it was too late.

"Laura, I'm sure you've been all the family he needs. I remember Frank speaking very highly of you, how proud he was to have you as his. I'd be honored to watch over your son. I'll grab some more details from you in a bit and I'll go find him later and introduce myself. Even though Frank was a Charon, I can't promise you Jake'll end up one. It doesn't work like that. If I think he'd be a good fit, I'll invite him to come hang out at the clubhouse, but from there, it's a club decision on whether he gets voted in or not. Either way, I promise you I'll keep my eye on him. Make sure he's doing okay. Can you give me some more details about what's going on with you? How long you think you've got left?"

"Frank never did mean it. It wasn't his fault, not really."

Ah, fuck. I had a good idea where this story was going. So many veterans suffered with mental illness. Post Traumatic Stress Disorder in particular, could make them violent and abusive.

"I'm sorry none of us picked up on the fact he'd grown violent. We would have stepped in."

She winced and shook her head, gaining my full attention.

"Laura, be straight with me on this. Was Frank violent with you before he came home with PTSD?"

She sighed and closed her eyes before she slowly nodded her head. "But it got a lot worse after he retired. He took to drinking, which led to him lashing out more often." She cleared her throat and lifted her iced tea to take a sip as her cheeks grew pink.

"Laura, that ain't nothing to be ashamed of. I only wish I'd known so something could have been done to help you. We maybe could have stepped in, gotten him help. Given you some support."

She quickly wiped her eyes. "Oh, you are a sweet man. And I know it's partly my fault. I never came around the club or got to know any of you. That's on me. But I fear there wasn't anything anyone could have done that would have changed who Frank was. Sadly, it seems he lashed out one too many times. At least, that's what my doctors say might be the cause of the brain tumor. They're going in to operate, but there's no guarantee on how these things will turn out."

Guilt was burning me from the inside out. Frank had been physically abusing his wife and none of us had known. None of us had fucking cared enough to make sure he was taking care of his fucking family like he should have been. Fuck.

"When is the surgery?"

"Not until the new year. Hopefully over the next few months you can build a rapport with my boy? So if I don't come out of it, he's got some support. I'll rest easier knowing I'm not leaving him all alone."

I took her hand between my palms and held her gaze. "I promise you I'll take care of your boy, and if you ever need anything else, you call me and we'll get it taken care of, okay? It doesn't matter how small or big, you call me."

She teared up again as she nodded and I pulled a card free to give her so she had my number.

"Right, so tell me where we can find this son of yours so we can see about bringing him into the fold."

Chapter 1

Early August 2018
Bash

Never had I said no to Scout, the president of the Charon MC.

About two years ago, when he approached me and asked if I wanted to come hang out with the Charon MC I'd said yes, and I'd been saying it ever since. But after the past several hours, I was beginning to wonder if maybe I shouldn't start saying no once in a while. Not that Scout actually asked if I wanted to come on this run. He'd just told me I was joining Mac, Arrow and Tiny on a trip up to New York and that Mac was in the lead. That had been yesterday. Then, first thing this morning, he drove us to the airport in Houston and I officially left Texas for the first time in my life.

Staten Island, New York was nothing like Bridgewater, Texas. Not the landscape, not the people. A club by the name of the Satan's Knights was hosting us. A young prospect, Nico, had come and picked us up from the airport before taking us to a house where we were greeted by a tatted-up half-naked man who was hung over as hell. Parrish eventually got some coffee into him and Mac and Arrow had explained why we were there, which had come with a nice little lesson on Charon MC history.

The simple reason for our trip was that the Ice Riders MC up in Boston had sent two men down to Bridgewater to get our attention. Stupid bastards chose to do that by holding Mac, Tiny and Scout's women hostage. Marie, Scout's old lady, had been eight months pregnant and the trauma had sent her into early labor. Thank fuck both Marie and little Joey were both going to be just fine. But no one was happy with what had gone down. So Scout had reached out to Parrish to ask if he could give us a place to stay while we investigated how to deal with the club that had declared war on us.

But nothing in life was ever simple.

Turned out this fucking mess was a massive web that involved us all: The Charons, Satan's Knights, Ice Riders, along with the L.A. mob and a cartel here in New York. That's how I now found myself in the back of a car with Mac and Riggs, a Satan's Knight, heading to a bank to collect ledgers.

Those fucking ledgers had been the bane of the Charon MC since September, 2016. Before he died in the 9/11 attacks on New York, John Bennett, the brother of our VP Bulldog, had spent his time collecting information on several different organizations. Stupid fucker detailed it all in the ledgers. One on each organization. The only one who'd known about them before John's death had been Antonia Sabella, the head of the L.A. mob. The only reason he'd known was because John hadn't just collected information on them, he'd stolen money and destroyed their records of contacts and other things. Sabella had been mad as hell, and we assume had been coming after John when he'd died.

Then, just before the fifteenth anniversary of the attacks, it was discovered a few bags had missed United flight 175, which had crashed into the south tower. John's carry-on bag had been one of them. For some reason, he'd been forced to check the bag, and it had missed the flight. Sabella had wanted that bag, but the only way to get it was to use John's only remaining family. A daughter who'd been sent to live with her uncle after her parents had died on that plane.

Silk hadn't wanted to know about the bag or anything else to do with the anniversary, but Sabella hadn't cared. He'd taken her and used her to get the bag released from LAX. He didn't count on Silk being so damn smart, though. Or the fact that airport employees would recognize him and want to help Silk. They got her into a private room to open her father's bag and she found so much more than simply one ledger on the L.A. Mob. John had stashed six ledgers in that damn bag. Seeing as I was only a lowly prospect, I didn't know everything about them but I paid attention to what was said around me. And I'd spent a lot of time working behind the bar in the clubhouse. You could learn a hell of a lot by just staying quiet and listening to talk around a bar. I picked up who each of those books had been on. Charon MC, Iron Hammers MC, Satan's Cowboys MC, Ice Riders MC, L.A. mob and N.Y. mob.

In the aftermath of that trip to LAX, it was also revealed that John had made copies of his ledgers and hidden them around the country in safe deposit boxes. Each book had a key, address and box number inside of it. As far as I knew, the boxes here in New York were the only ones left now.

The boxes we were on the way to empty would contain the Ice Riders and the N.Y. mob books. Parrish had been keen to get a look at the mob one. Apparently, here in New York it wasn't a single mob kinda deal, but five families, plus cartels. None of us knew exactly who John had gotten information on. Parrish was hopeful it was a cartel that was currently screwing with the Satan's Knights.

The way the L.A. mob fit in to this mess was that the Rider we'd questioned told us his club had been having trouble with a cartel in New York, and Sabella had reached out to them, telling them if they came down and dealt with us, he'd give the Riders what they needed to deal with the cartel.

Like I said, turned out this shit was one, big, tangled web.

"Right, here we are. Let's go get those ledgers."

Keeping my place behind Mac and Riggs, I kept my head down and constantly glanced around us at everything that was going on. There were so many people everywhere, it was insane. We finally made it into the bank and up to the service desk. Mac pulled out all the paperwork and handed it over. I rather liked the efficiency. Guess with so many customers these big city banks had things streamlined. Before we knew it, we were in a private viewing room with three boxes. Like I said, as a prospect, I didn't know everything. For example, I'd had no fucking clue that John had left an extra box at each location. Clearly, Mac had expected to find the extra box since he had a form signed by Silk to give us access to it. The thing was linked to the other boxes, but couldn't be accessed with only the key. It was set up so only Silk could get it, or someone acting on her behalf.

Riggs set an empty bag on the table.

"Right. Let's empty these babies and get back to Kate's so we can go through them properly."

We each took a box. I ended up with the Ice Rider's box, Riggs, the mob's, and Mac, Silk's. I grabbed the ledger from my box and shoved it into the bag, as did Riggs. My eyes bugged out of my head when Mac opened his box up.

"Fuck."

Mac just nodded at my curse and started moving it all into Riggs' bag. There were copies of the two ledgers, and also a letter to Claudine, which was Silk's real name. But on top of that were a few rolls of $100 bills and a Glock with a spare clip.

"John left a box like this at each location. It's a failsafe for Silk, in case she was in trouble. The letter will, no doubt, be like the others, telling her to get away from whoever has forced her here and then go to her uncle for protection. I'll make sure the letter and cash get back to Silk. We'll leave the gun with you, Riggs."

"Good deal. Let's get the fuck outta here."

Mac took the bag and held it out to me. "Scout's orders, Bash. You're officially on guard duty. Your job, as long as these ledgers exist, is to make sure they're safe."

I grunted at the weight of the bag that now had four fucking ledgers in it, plus the gun and cash.

With a laugh, Riggs slapped me on the back. Hard.

"Our very own Moses. Classic."

Not really sure were this guy got this *Moses* business from. But damnit, I'd just been made a guardian to a bunch of old books.

Fuck my life.

Seriously, I really needed to start saying no to Scout on occasion.

Riggs started speaking as we rolled up in front of a bar.

"A while back, an asshole blew up our old clubhouse. After that, we were operating out of Pipe's garage until I came across this gem. Now, we call this place home."

Sign over the door stated it was Big Nose Kate's. What a fucking weird name for a bar. I followed Mac and Riggs through the door, looking forward to being able to sit down. The bag weighed a fucking ton. Three steps in, I froze for a moment. The place was packed. Just before we'd left Parrish's place earlier, he'd gotten a call from his daughter, saying their house had been broken into while she and her little brother were sleeping upstairs. The Satan's Knights were on lockdown, which meant everyone the club cared about was heading this way. By the looks of it, most, if not all of them, were already here.

There was only one chick behind the bar and she was running to keep up. Woman was hot. Bit on the skinny side, but with the most beautiful wavy, honey golden hair. I couldn't tell her eye color from this far away, but the straight line of her nose and the smile she gave the guy she was serving had my heart rate picking up. Maybe having to hang around here to guard these books wasn't going to be such a bad thing after all. I wondered if she'd mind if I jumped behind the bar and helped her out? I'd just stash the bag behind there somewhere, where I could see it.

I finally caught sight of Arrow and Tiny sitting down at the far end of the bar with a few of the Knights, so I started to head over their way. But Riggs stopped me.

"Sorry, kid. We don't get to be social yet. Need to go through those books of yours."

Withholding a sigh, I followed him down a narrow hallway to an office. Mac came with us and once I set the bag down, he opened it up and handed off the Glock and clip to Riggs.

"Those boxes were at least seventeen years old. You'll want to thoroughly check over that weapon before anyone tries to fire it."

Riggs took it and examined it quickly. "Serial number has been filed off. We'll take care of it."

Pulling out a drawer, he dropped both the gun and clip in before shutting it. "Now, these ledgers. Let me take the mob one. We're looking for any reference to the Sinaloa cartel."

Mac grabbed the Ice Riders ledger and I had no clue what they wanted me to do. The other two books were just copies of what they were going to look over.

"I couldn't help but notice your bartender out there is looking rushed. Since you two have this covered, why don't I go out and give her a hand? I'll take back over guard duty when Mac's done."

Riggs winced and rubbed the back of his neck. "Yeah, Nico is supposed to be helping her but he's busy dealing with Parrish. You know what you're doing out there?"

"One of my main jobs with the Charons is manning the club bar. I know what to do."

Riggs looked to Mac, who nodded. "All right then, out you go. Tell Lydia I sent you to help her so she should fucking play nice."

Well, that was encouraging.

Before going out to the bar, I slipped into the men's room and pulled my phone out. To make this run, I'd had to leave my ma home with nothing more than some hired help. She had early onset Alzheimer's and was getting worse. New York was a long fucking way from Texas and I was nervous as hell being so far from her. I'd paid Beth, a home nurse, to be there as close to 24/7 as I could afford, but that shit didn't come cheap so there were times Ma was going to be alone while I was gone. I hated that. Hated I couldn't be there for her. I also felt guilty as fuck, because part of me was excited to be getting away for a little while. I'd been feeling like I was suffocating under all the responsibility for a while now. So when Scout had announced I'd be coming on this trip, a part of me had been elated to be getting a break from it all.

I shot off a text to Beth, asking how Ma was doing and she got straight back to me, saying she was doing as well as normal. My heart was lighter for having confirmation Ma was okay as I made my way out to the main room, which was even busier now. Lifting the hatch, I went behind the bar and moved up to Lydia, who turned to glare at me. Fuck, she really was gorgeous. Her green eyes were currently spitting fire, but they were stunning. I spoke before she could.

"Hey, darlin', Riggs told me to come give you a hand."

Her expression cooled slightly. "He did, did he? 'Bout fucking time. Okay, cowboy, you ever worked in a bar before?"

I grabbed a glass and pulled a perfect beer before setting it on the bar top. "Been working the clubhouse bar for a few years now, darlin'. Don't you worry, I can keep up."

She gave me a nod. "Excellent. You take that half of the bar. What you see is what we've got. We don't do anything fancy. If you notice anything getting low, let me know."

With that, I turned and tried to ignore how hot the chick working beside me was as I served various Knights and their families. Over the next hour or so, various Knights went back to join Mac and Riggs before returning to the bar. Then Parrish made his entrance with his arm wrapped around a woman who must be his wife. A little boy ran straight up to her, and when she picked him up like it was the most natural thing in the world, I released a breath I didn't realize I'd been holding.

Scout had told us before we came up here that Parrish's wife, Reina, had been in a car accident that had left her with a five year gap in her memory. She hadn't been able to remember her husband or her son. Considering most days my own mother didn't know who the hell I was, that got to me. Seeing the way she was with her boy, Danny, right now, gave me hope that unlike my own mother, Reina was starting to remember her life. That Danny wouldn't have to live with the knowledge the woman at the center of his world didn't know who he was half the time.

Clearing my throat, I turned my focus back to pouring drinks. I didn't need to be getting fucking emotional in the middle of the Knights' clubhouse. Wolf followed

Parrish in and called church. Mac came out with the bag of fucking books for me.

"You're back on duty, Bash. Need you out from behind the bar."

I gave Lydia an apologetic look. "Sorry, sugar. Duty calls."

She shrugged. "Always does. Tell Nico to get his ass back here, would you?"

"Sure, babe."

After pouring myself a beer, I took the damn bag and moved out from behind the bar. After finding Nico and telling him Lydia needed him, I made myself at home at an out of the way at a table in the corner, with the bag sitting on the timber in front of me.

Still couldn't quite believe I was stuck guarding a bunch of old books. That I couldn't even help behind the bar while I did it.

Once church was out, Riggs came over to my table with his laptop in hand.

"Hey, Moses. We got some more work to do."

"Do we need to go back to the office again?"

"Nah, here'll work. Just let me grab a fucking drink."

Despite how many people were here, the corner I'd found wasn't too noisy, and our backs were to the wall so no one would be able to sneak a look over our shoulders without our knowing about it. I watched as, on his way to the bar, Riggs stopped by a table where two boys were sitting down coloring, while a woman stood next to them swaying as she held a newborn wrapped in a blue blanket. He slipped up behind the sexy brunette and in one smooth move, grabbed her hips and pulled her back against him while he shoved his face in against her throat. With a laugh, she turned in his arms so she could kiss his lips. Wolf whistles filled the air as his club brothers started to stir him up over always being on his old lady.

The older boy looked up at his mother's laugh and jumped out of his seat with an excited "Daddy!", running straight for Riggs. With a grin, I took another mouthful of beer. What would that be like? To have a woman and kids who looked at you the way Riggs' did. He picked up his son and spoke too quietly for me to hear before he pressed a kiss to the top of his head and sat him back at the table. Then, after another kiss for his old lady, and one for each of his other two sons, he headed to the bar. He returned to my table with a glass of amber liquid and set about booting up his laptop.

"Moses, pull out the Riders' ledger for me." He paused to down half his glass in one shot. Grabbing a pen and a paper napkin, he wrote some dates down. "Mark these pages for me. I just gotta find this fucking lawyer for Parrish, then we'll chase down those addresses."

Pulling out both copies of the Ice Riders' ledger, I flipped through to the appropriate pages then swiveled them to face Riggs.

"What's with the Moses thing? You know my name is Bash, right?"

With a smirk, he leaned back to take a drink. Then gave me a brief glance before he returned his gaze to the screen.

"You're not Catholic are you?"

I shrugged, not seeing the point. "Ma took me to a few Baptist services when I was a kid. What's your point?"

He shook his head. "God entrusted Moses with the Ten Commandments. He had to guard the stone tablets they were written on… You seeing the similarities yet?"

Man played the fool well, but Riggs was no dummy.

I rolled my eyes before nodding at the books. "Sure. But I don't think these things are on the same level."

Riggs barked out a laugh. "Close enough."

Before he could say more, his laptop dinged and he got serious. "Found the fucker." He looked up around the room until his eyes caught Parrish's gaze. With a nod, he came over to us.

"You found him?"

"Sure did. Fucker is living it up over at the Playboy Club in Manhattan." He grabbed another napkin and wrote out the address. "I'll set you guys up with a membership that should get you in the door."

Parrish reached out and squeezed his shoulder. "Thanks, brother."

Then he marched off, grabbing Wolf and the vice president, Pipe, before heading out the door. I finished my beer and decided to grab a fresh one while Riggs did his thing.

"Want another drink?"

21

"Sure. Lydia knows my poison."

Chapter 2

It was mid-morning the following day when Nico came through the door calling out "Honey, we're home!" to announce Scout's arrival. The rest of the Charons and I were sitting together at the bar with cups of coffee, me with this fucking bag of books under my arm that rested on the bar top. Scout came straight over to us, looking like he was ready to get shit done.

Arrow greeted him first. "Hey, prez. Good to see you."

Scout gave us each a back slap before he faced Arrow. "Anything new happen since my early morning phone call from Wolf?"

Arrow nodded. "Plenty. We were waiting on you to come in before church was called."

He'd barely finished speaking when Wolf's shrill whistle filled the air.

"Get your asses to church. Charons, too."

But even here, that didn't include me. Normally a man did twelve months as a prospect before he earned his full colors. It'd been two fucking years since I became a prospect for the Charon MC and these constant reminders that I still didn't have a place at the big boys' table fucking stunk. It's not like I hadn't earned my patch. Hell, I'd even taken a bullet when I was assigned guarding Mac's old lady, Zara. Of course, by taking said bullet, I'd been taken out and the bad guys had managed to get their hands on Zara, so I didn't bring that shit up with anyone.

While everyone of importance was back in church, I sat with my bag of books and sipped my coffee while I watched Lydia restocking the bar. The longer I watched her ass, the more uncomfortable I got sitting there in my jeans. Considering I wasn't allowed to leave the ledgers to help her behind the bar, I was pretty sure I'd get my ass handed to me if I left them to go make a pass at her. And that was a damn shame, because not only was Lydia pretty as all get out, she was seriously stressed and could use a good fuck to help her relax.

A sudden influx of noise had me looking toward the door that led back to the chapel just in time to see all the men returning, all getting ready to ride out. Scout beelined for me and I inwardly cringed at the look on his face. Whatever he was about to tell me, he thought I wasn't going to like it. He was probably right.

"Bash, you're staying put." He stood in close so only I'd hear his words. "Don't take this personally, Jake. It's not because I don't think you're capable of handling this run. It's because you shouldn't have to. We're going to take out the Ice Riders, son. It's gonna get messy and you're too young to have to see that shit if you don't have to."

I wanted to call bullshit. I was twenty-five fucking years old. Men my age were off fighting the war, seeing bloodshed every damn day.

"Don't fight it, Jake. I still need you to watch over those ledgers. Can you imagine if the wrong people got a hold of them? Worked out there were more? We'd have all sorts of fuckers gunning for Silk and the club. Keeping them safe is important."

He didn't need to say what his eyes were telling me. I was just like those fucking ledgers. Something he wanted kept safe.

Fuck it all.

I clenched my jaw so I didn't say something to my president I'd most likely regret later, and gave the man a nod. Scout spun on his heel and headed out. I stared at my hands, clenching and unclenching my fists as I seethed over being fucking left behind yet again.

"Looks like you could use a drink, cowboy. Beer, or you want something stronger?"

"Stronger. Definitely something stronger."

When a glass with a couple of fingers of amber liquid appeared beside my hands, I looked up and straight into her green eyes. She held me captive for a minute with her gaze and I got the impression she was seeing more than I wanted her to. Someone else called for her attention, and she looked away, breaking the contact before she moved. As the sound of Harleys filled the air, I snatched the glass and threw back the contents faster than I should have. The burn had my eyes watering, but I thankfully managed to hold in the cough that would have made me look like a fucking pussy to the few who were left in the bar.

It was hours later when the men rolled back in, celebrating. Scout came over to me, with Riggs at his side.

"Bash, good news. We can burn these fuckers to ash and you're free to enjoy some down time. I'll take the bag with the cash."

"C'mon, Moses, got a barrel out the back we can use."

After pulling the four ledgers from the bag, I handed it to Scout. Then, once I was off the bar stool, Riggs slapped my back.

"Let's get this shit done so we can throw back a few drinks. Gonna get wild tonight. You mind jumping in and helping Lydia again?"

I shrugged as we headed out to the barrel. "Sure. Don't suppose you know when we're heading home?"

"Scout's got you boys booked in on a flight in the morning, I believe. Wasn't room tonight, although he did get his own ass a flight home."

I nodded. "He's got a preemie baby to worry about. I get why he wants to be home."

Riggs grabbed a can of gas and indicated I toss the ledgers in a rusty old metal barrel. It was just the two of us out here as everyone else was already starting to party inside.

"What's got you wanting to race back? Got an old lady stashed away back home?"

I laughed. "Nah, only woman waiting on me is my ma, and she'll probably not remember who I am anyhow."

He winced. "Sorry to hear that, Moses."

Riggs sprinkled the gas over the ledgers before he lit a match and flicked it into the barrel. The skin on my face got a blast of heat as the flames whooshed to life.

I'm not sure why I kept talking. I liked Riggs, even if he did insist on calling me that stupid ass name.

"She's got early onset Alzheimer's. Getting worse. I swear, I spend more time pretending to be my old man than I do being myself around her."

"Where's your old man?"

"Dead. Killed himself back in 2014. Came back from war with PTSD, and he never got better."

"Fuck, man."

Yep. Pretty much. There wasn't really a lot you could say to that.

"I've got a nurse staying with Ma, she's doing okay, but I want to get back and make sure. You know?"

"Yeah, I get it." He cleared his throat and looked into the barrel. "Well, those fuckers are nothing but ash now. Let's go get you a drink before I put you to work."

The job was done and it was nearly time to go home. Scout had already left for the airport, but as Riggs had told me, he hadn't been able to get us all on the flight, so while he headed back to his wife, daughter and newborn son, the rest of us got to spend another night in New York. Not that I was complaining. Since the fucking ledgers had been incinerated, I was finally free from my guard duty over them and was able to focus on more enjoyable things. Like Lydia.

It was early morning and everyone had either headed home or upstairs to crash for the night. It had been a crazy night at Big Nose Kate's with so many of us celebrating. The place had been over-the-top busy, so Riggs had asked me to help behind the bar, and I'd jumped at the chance. Put me nice and close to Lydia, who I was free to make a pass at now. I'd continued to hang back as the others had slowly left, and now it was just her and me.

I went over and flipped the lock on the door before returning behind the bar, where Lydia was wiping things down and tidying up. Facing away from me, with one hand braced on the counter behind the bar, she stretched to put a bottle on a high shelf. My gaze ate up the sight of her lithe body, the line of her sexy curves and the peek of pale skin revealed due to her shirt lifting up. My cock kicked behind my fly as I slid up behind her. Resting one palm on her left hip, I ran my other hand up her right arm, taking the bottle and easily returning it to its place.

She stiffened and her breath hitched as I took her palm that had held the bottle in mine, and guided it to the back of my neck before I trailed my fingers down the soft, sensitive skin of her inner arm.

"You sure are pretty, darlin'."

I emphasized my southern drawl and finished by pressing a kiss to the side of her temple and taking a deep breath of her sweet scent. When she didn't push me away, or tell me to fuck off, I took that as a sign she'd been feeling me too. I let my fingers continue down, over the side of her breast and down her rib cage. She was damn skinny, not an ounce of fat on her, but before I could get caught up with worrying about her eating habits, she moaned and with a wriggle of her hips, had my full attention. When she slipped her fingers up into my hair, scraping her fingernails over my scalp, she had me groaning as a shiver wracked through my body. Her hand not in my hair slid over my hip before her fingers curled into the back pocket of my jeans and pulled me in tight against her sexy ass.

Nuzzling against the side of her face, I made my way down past her ear and kissed a path over her jaw and down to her throat. She tasted as good as she smelled, and I wanted more. Glancing down her front, I could see her nipples had gone rock-hard beneath her thin shirt.

"Those for me, darlin'?"

I reached up and gave each little nub a tweak through her shirt and she wriggled her ass against my hard cock in response.

"Ain't no one else here, cowboy. Who do you think they're for?"

She wasn't some meek and mild woman. Nope, Lydia was full of sass. With a growl, I grabbed the bottom of her shirt and lifted it up over her tits, revealing a lacy black bra. Since she didn't release her hold on me so I could take the thing off, I left it bunched up above her tits and slid my palms inside the cups. She was a perfect little handful, and desperate to see them, I lifted each soft mound from its confines, exposing hard, dusky pink nipples to my gaze, and my mouth watered for a taste of them. Without shifting my gaze from her, I took each nipple between a thumb and finger and rolled them, fucking loving how she squirmed against me with each roll or tweak I gave her. I teased her with tugs and flicks until she was rubbing her thighs together and groaning. When I pulled away from her, her palms slipped free from my hair and pocket. I made fast work of flicking open her bra, spinning her around and stripping her from the waist up.

"Fuck, sugar…"

I didn't give her any more words, just grabbed her hips and lifted her onto the counter before wrapping my mouth around one of those tight buds. With a moan, I curled my tongue around it, getting it nice and wet before I scraped my teeth lightly over the hard little nub. With a gasp, her fingers dove into my hair, gripping me tightly to her as I continued to tease her. The tit not in my mouth I had in my palm, kneading her flesh and tweaking the nipple, getting her nice and worked up. Her little mewls and groans had me on edge. I could feel the pre-cum leaking from my cock, dampening my briefs.

With a curse, I released her, and cupping her face in my palms, I took her lips in a hard kiss. She opened up beneath me and I took the invitation and invaded her mouth, thrusting my tongue in like I wanted to do with my cock in her pussy. She shifted her hands to my shirt, tugging it up my torso before she dragged those sexy as fuck nails over my hard abs.

She broke the kiss.

"Lose the shirt, babe."

I took half a step back and started to shrug out of my cut. The cool air of the room rushed in between us, and as though she just remembered where we were, Lydia put her palms over her tits as she glanced around the room.

"Ain't nobody here but me, and I locked the door, darlin'. But if it makes you feel better…"

I took my cut and wrapped it around behind her, helping her thread her arms into it. It was huge on her but fuck, did it suit her. Having my name on her made me a little wild. I bit my tongue against telling her she was mine, that I'd get her a cut of her own declaring she was my property. Fuck, I wasn't even a patched in brother. And I wasn't from New York. What the fuck was I thinking? That she was gonna move down south with me? Riggs would probably have my balls if I took his best worker from him.

Fingers pulling at my belt had my runaway thoughts back where they should be and in a quick move, I had my shirt over my head and on the floor. Lydia's eyes went wide as her gaze traced the ink over my shoulder and down my arm before she slipped off the counter. Leaning into me, she licked over my nipple and gave it nip as she finished with my belt and popped the top button. I grabbed a handful of her dark honey-colored curls and tilted her face up to me as she slid my fly down and slipped her warm hand inside to rub over the hard length waiting there for her.

"You want me as bad as I want you, dontcha, darlin'? You been watching me while I've been watching you, haven't you?"

"Maybe."

With a wink, she slipped her fingers under the waistband of my briefs and pushed them, together with my jeans, over my hips, releasing my hard cock from the confines of my clothes. It slapped against my stomach before she wrapped her soft fingers around it. My eyes nearly rolled all the way back into my skull at how fucking good it felt when she firmly stroked me.

"Fuck, darlin'."

Taking her mouth in another hard kiss, I grabbed at her jeans, fumbling in my rush to get to her flesh. But it didn't slow me down. I had those fuckers undone and shoved down in seconds. I slipped my palm over the skin I'd just revealed. Over her soft, smooth pussy that was shaved clean and oh, so fucking wet. Continuing to kiss her, I slid my fingers through her cream, teasing her for a few moments before I finally thrust two fingers inside her pussy.

With a gasp, she broke from the kiss and I nearly went to my knees with how her body clenched around my fingers. I couldn't fucking wait to get my cock into her tight heat. Her hands went back to my dick, one stroking while the other went lower, cupping my balls. It didn't take long for her to get me worked up to the edge. Fuck, it felt so damn good but I was not coming in her hands. Not this time. After one last thrust with my fingers, I slid free from her body, making sure I slid over her clit on my way out. Then I stepped back, pulling my cock from her hands as I did.

Looking her in the eye, I raised my fingers and licked them clean, enjoying the taste of her cream.

"You taste good, darlin'. And I'll get me some more of that later, but right now, I need in you. You good with that?"

She nodded and kicked off her heels before pulling one leg free of the material in record time. I pulled my wallet out and grabbed the condom before returning it to my jeans. Tearing the packet open, I had myself gloved up and my palms wrapped around Lydia's hips in record time. Lifting her once more on the counter, I shifted her so she was sitting on the edge before I took a moment to take her in. Her green eyes flashed with hunger, her chest heaved with her every breath, making her so fucking pretty—tits thrust up toward me with each inhale. I'd be making those bounce for me real soon. And her pussy, fuck. She really was gorgeous.

"So fucking pretty."

Taking my cock in my palm, I shifted in, lined up and thrust in deep. I held still for a minute, just enjoying the way she fit around me. She'd wrapped her legs around my waist and her arms around my neck, her fingers back in my hair as she nipped at my jaw.

"Fuck me already, Bash. Quit teasing."

"This ain't teasing, darlin'. I'm just taking my time to enjoy this."

I pulled my hips back, loving how she shuddered before I thrust in deep again. Palming one of her tits, and flicking her nipple with my thumb, I took her mouth with mine, tangling my tongue with hers. I'd never get enough of her taste.

When the door banged open behind me. We both froze. Fuck. I was certain I'd locked it.

Chapter 3

"Whoa. Moses, you dirty dog," Riggs cheered. Glancing over my shoulder at the self-proclaimed tiger, I watched as he crossed his arms against his chest. A grin spread across his face and amusement flickered in his eyes before a serious expression settled over his features. "You got that shit wrapped, right?" He paused for a second, clearly lost in thought. "Or not. It all depends on the outcome you want. I mean, the first time I fucked my Kitten, I obviously didn't glove up and it turned out to be the best thing I ever did."

I honestly couldn't believe this was happening and when Lydia groaned, I knew I wasn't the only one. I was basically frozen in shock as Riggs called me that stupid fucking name he'd given me, then went on about how he knocked up his woman the first time he got her under him, like stopping to chat with a man you'd walked in on having sex was completely fucking normal behavior.

Lydia buried her face in against my neck and pressed her body up against mine as close as she could, hiding herself. I was extra glad I'd put my cut on her now. I glared over my shoulder at the smiling fucker who just stood there with his arms crossed, watching us like a perv.

"Are you fucking serious right now, Riggs? Get outta here."

With a laugh, he put his palms up in surrender. "Hey, news flash, kid. You're the one fucking in the middle of my bar. If you wanted privacy, you should've taken her upstairs, or at least banged her in the kitchen. Ain't none of us going in there. Well, maybe Wolf, but it's way past that old cat's bedtime."

"You should be damn grateful I had to catch the fucking plane up here so I'm not carrying right now."

He laughed as he started to back away.

"Word to the wise, man, we all got a key to this place. If you don't want an audience, move the show to another room. But, hey, if that's your kink, I got some killer video equipment and I hear PornHub offers a dime piece for a decent fuck. We can make you the next fucking prince of porn."

With that, he grabbed his phone off the end of the bar and turned back toward the door and was gone.

"I cannot believe this is happening."

I pressed a kiss against her forehead before I reluctantly pulled my still hard cock from the warmth of her pussy.

"How about we move this upstairs?"

She looked flustered and embarrassed. "Don't worry about Riggs, darlin'. He'll give me shit over this but I'll make sure he don't say a word to you about it."

She shook her head as she slipped off the counter and pulled her panties and jeans back on. "The whole club'll know by morning, Bash."

I couldn't decide if that fact upset her. After dealing with the condom, I kept my gaze down as I pulled my briefs and jeans up.

"You regret hooking up with me?"

Fuck, I felt like I was a teenager right now. Before I could figure out a way to get the fuck out of the room, she was pressed up against my front, the leather of my cut the only thing between us.

"Bash." She paused and shoved her face under mine, into my line of sight, cupping my jaw so I had to look at her. I began to relax when I couldn't see pity or anger in her gaze. "I don't regret hooking up with you, just the location. And the fact there was no happy ending for either of us."

That had me smirking. "You want your happy ending, huh?"

She shrugged and tried to back away. I wrapped my arms around her, keeping her close.

"Well, what the lady wants, the lady gets."

Taking her hand, I led her upstairs and into a spare room. This time I shut the door then shoved a chair under the damn knob. No one was interrupting us this time. I tossed the shirt I'd grabbed off the floor of the bar in the direction of my bag and toed off my boots, sending them in the same direction before I turned my attention back to Lydia. My gut dropped at the sight of her there, standing by the bed, holding my cut closed over her chest as she eyed the door.

"Hey, Lydia, if you've changed your mind, that's cool."

I moved toward the door, to shift the chair, when her warm palm wrapped around my wrist.

"Don't. I haven't changed my mind. I, ah, I just got nervous about you seeing me."

Turning toward her, I cupped her face between my palms, forcing her to look me in the eyes. I saw in her gaze she was being real with me. She honestly had an issue with how she looked.

"I got a good look and feel downstairs, darlin', and there wasn't a damn thing about you I found lacking."

Before she could say anything else, I took her mouth in mine, kissing her deeply until she relaxed against me. I kept my mouth on hers as I peeled my cut from her shoulders. Running my hands over her soft skin, I couldn't get enough. With a groan, I pulled from her mouth and kissed my way down her throat. Her fingers curled around the top of my jeans before she once more opened them up and freed my rock-hard cock. I nearly ripped her jeans in my attempt to get them off her. She chuckled as she wriggled her hips as I dragged them down her legs. Once she was naked, I shoved my own pants down and kicked them over toward my bag.

I wrapped an arm around her waist and pulled her back in tight against me, taking her mouth with mine before she could think about the fact she was naked. I didn't want her stressing out over a damn thing. I slid my free hand down her body, tweaking a nipple before caressing her flat stomach and down to her pussy. A groan slipped out when I cupped her bare mound in my palm and found her hot and wet. I nipped at her jaw as I slid one finger inside her heat. Her fingers dug into my shoulders as she thrust her hips into my hand. After slipping a second finger inside her slick core, I began pumping my fingers in and out, pressing my thumb over her clit as she got closer to climaxing. When she was right on the edge, moaning and writhing against me, I pulled my hand away.

Her growl was cute as fuck, but before she could attack me for stopping, I scooped her up and dropped her on the bed.

"Spread those legs, darlin', I wanna taste."

I gave my cock a couple of solid strokes as I watched her do as she was told. I knew she was so close to coming she could taste it, was desperate for it. With a grin, I pressed my knee to the mattress before I dropped down over her and covered her pussy with my mouth. The first lick up her center had my eyes rolling back before I closed them to focus on getting as much of her honey as I could. She tasted fucking divine and I wanted it all.

She ran a palm over my head, trying to hold me to her. Like I was going anywhere? With a growl, I thrust my tongue in deep and when she started to wriggle around, I placed my palm over her tummy to hold her still. I wasn't even nearly done with this. Another long lick through her pussy lips and up to her clit had her crying out. When I thrust two fingers back inside her core and suckled her hard little clit, she blew apart, bucking against me as she gave me her cream. I stayed where I was, lapping up everything she gave me before bringing her down from this first high of the night.

I rose over her and grinned as she lay there, a sheen of sweat on her skin as she panted. Her eyes were closed and a sweet little smile was curling her slightly parted lips.

"Don't go to sleep on me, sugar. I'm not nearly done with you."

It felt like I'd only just closed my eyes when someone pounding on the door had me awake again.

"Fuck."

"Bash! Time to get up. We roll out in ten."

"I'll be right out!"

Mac's voice was not a welcome greeting to my morning. However, the empty bed beside me was even less so. Guess I must have slept for longer than I thought if Lydia had had time to sneak out on me. Fuck, I'd been looking forward to another round this morning. Although, with only ten minutes to get ready, I wouldn't have had time. It would be a crime to fuck that gorgeous woman that fast. Not to mention a waste.

Dragging my ass outta bed, I pulled my jeans on and sat down to deal with my socks and boots. Standing up, I stretched out my back and neck. I needed more sleep. I was so fucking tired. Not that I regretted the reason behind my tiredness. Not one bit. In fact, I'd happily do it again in a heartbeat.

Grabbing my t-shirt, I put it on before finally grabbing my cut. As I slid it over my shoulders a waft of Lydia's scent washed over me, making me groan as my cock sprang to life. Fuck. Twisting my head, I pressed my nose to the leather. With my eyes closed, I took a deep breath, catching more of her scent from when I'd put the leather on her last night. Memories of all the ways I'd taken her filled my mind and made my cock throb for some attention.

Noise on the other side of the door pulled me from my thoughts. Fuck my life. There was no time to even take care of myself. With a wince, I adjusted my hard cock so it wasn't pressed against the zipper of my jeans. I grabbed a beanie from my bag before I stuffed yesterday's clothes back into it, zipped it up and slung it over my shoulder. I opened the door and as I stepped out into the main room, I slipped the hat over my head. Wolf-whistles and laughter filled the room.

"Shut it." Heat flared over my cheeks and I knew they'd turned red.

"Naw, c'mon, man. Sounds like you had a great night. We're just congratulating you on it."

Mac smirked at me while Tiny gave me a shoulder bump. Arrow was also smirking as he zipped his own bag.

Mac's phone dinged. "Nico's waiting on us downstairs. We'll get coffee at the airport. No time now."

Damn, that meant I wouldn't even have time to go searching downstairs to see if Lydia was around for a goodbye kiss at least. Dammit. Following the others out, I kept my gaze scanning for any sign of her but didn't see her before we were loaded into a cage and Nico was driving us to the airport. Ignoring Nico's commentary, I scrubbed a hand over my face and tried to get my head in the game for what was waiting for me at home. Would Ma have even noticed I'd been gone? By the time I got home, I would have been gone about thirty-six hours. Only one night. Hopefully she hadn't gotten agitated with the change from normal.

Once we were through security and waiting at the gate, I shot off a text to Beth to let her know I was on my way back and to check on how Ma fared overnight. As always, Beth wrote straight back saying Ma was her usual self and she was happy I was coming home so soon. Not sure if it was Beth or Ma that was happy, but whatever.

Five hours later I was walking through the hot Texas air toward the Charon MC clubhouse. Mac, Tiny and Arrow were all grinning and clearly happy to be home but I just couldn't muster the energy to fake it. If anyone said anything, I'd blame it on being tired from my sleepless night, but in reality it was something so much more. After two years of doing all the shit prospect jobs and still not getting the reward of a full patch that I'd earned long ago, I was starting to lose faith in the club. In my place here within it.

By the time I filed in last through the door, Scout was there greeting us.

"Good to see you all got in safely. Sorry I couldn't get you home last night."

With a smirk, Arrow nudged me. "No problem, prez. Pretty sure it suited Bash, here, to have a few more hours in New York."

My face felt like it was on fire at Arrow announcing to the whole fucking room that I got some last night. Bastard.

"Oh, yeah?" Scout raised an eyebrow as he looked directly at me. Which just made my damn blush deepen. I was about to make a break for it when Scout moved to stand in front of me, cutting off my escape.

"Bash, all joking aside, you did good on this trip. We're having a barbecue later to celebrate. You're off the hook for any work. The other prospects can handle it all and you can sit back and enjoy the down time, yeah?"

My face started to cool down at the praise from the president, and the reward of not having to come straight back and have to work. I appreciated the break.

"Thanks, prez. Can I head off till then? I need to check in on my mother."

Scout gave me a nod. "Of course. Family always comes first."

As I made my way out to my bike I wondered if maybe I should have told Scout about what was going on with Ma. I hadn't said a word to anyone at the club about her condition or how badly she was deteriorating. I had no clue why I'd opened up a little to Riggs in New York last night, but he was the only one outside of doctors and nurses who knew about her having Alzheimer's.

The short ride home helped clear my head a little. Nothing like the open road and the roar of my Harley under me to wake me up and improve my mood. By the time I opened the front door to the house I shared with my mother, I had a smile on my face. It was getting late, well past Ma's usual dinner time, so I wasn't sure if she would still be up. I stepped through the door and Beth was there to greet me.

"Welcome home, Jake. Turned out to be a short trip, huh?"

I nodded. "Thankfully everything got handled quickly. How's Ma? She still awake?"

She gave me a sympathetic smile. "She turned in after dinner. She wanted to stay up to see you but got too tired. I promised her I'd stay to make sure you were whole and in one piece."

"So how old did she think I was?"

I wasn't sure where she was in her memories today, but if she was worried about me getting in whole and in one piece, I suspected she was thinking I was in my teens.

"Not entirely sure, but she mentioned high school. I need to get moving. I'm glad you're back. She's better when you're around. Even if she gets the dates mixed up, she knows who you are."

I gave her a quick hug. "Yeah, I know. It's just hard to wrap my head around not knowing who I'm supposed to be each time I see her."

She patted my cheek. "I know. It's always so hard on the families. The one with the disease is often the only one not suffering. They're back in the past, and happy."

"Until they have a good day, and they realize all they've missed out, all the hurt they've caused."

Sometimes the good days were nearly worse to witness than the bad days. Ma would get so upset that she was causing me so much pain with her either treating me like a young boy or thinking I was my old man.

Bidding Beth goodbye, I made my way up the stairs. After poking my head in to check that Ma was indeed safely asleep in her bed, I went onto my own room. I needed a couple hours of shuteye before I went back to the clubhouse for the celebration. By the time I'd stripped down, showered and crawled into bed, I'd decided I was going to skip the club barbecue. I needed sleep more than I needed to go back to the clubhouse and be given hell about my night with Lydia.

Chapter 4

I'd been back to real life for two fucking weeks and I was done with this shit. Ma was getting worse. Whenever she saw me, she'd either lay into me because, apparently it was all my fault I looked just like my old man, or she'd think I was my old man and try to talk me out of going away to war or some other thing. The only upside to this bitch of a disease my mother had was that, for increasing parts of her day, she forgot all about the final years of my father's life. Alzheimer's had done her a favor and removed all the drinking and yelling, all the beatings, the brain tumor. At this point it was a rare moment when she got that look in her eye that told me she was reliving one of those horrors.

"Frank? Where are you? Oh, there you are. Have you seen Jake? He should be home by now. You need to go look for him, make sure he's not getting into trouble with those hooligans he likes to hang out with. He knows better than to not be home in time for dinner."

I squeezed my eyes shut for a few moments and took a deep breath. Whenever my old man was home between deployments, I'd tried to make myself scarce. He'd always been a mean son of a bitch when he got in a mood, then after he'd been discharged from the military due to his PTSD, I'd put even more effort into staying out of his way. Anything was better than being yelled at and having to watch him slam around the house and beat on Ma. I'd been too young to stand up to him back then. Once, when I'd been in my late teens, I'd tried to stop him and copped a beating myself before he moved back on to Ma with more anger than before. Neither of us stood a fucking chance against him, and after that one go I had at him, Ma made me promise to not do anything like it again. So I dealt with it the only way I could think of—by avoiding the bastard. I still felt guilty about it, but I had no way to train so I could take him out. I guess I could have gotten my hands on a gun, but even then, I knew the chances of him getting the weapon and turning it on me or Ma were high. Ma had always thought I was out with friends, but normally I just sat down at the park in a dark corner and watched the others. At least that's what I'd done as a kid. When I was older, I'd sneak into bars to torture myself with wishing for shit I didn't think I'd ever be lucky enough to have, like good, solid friends that would have my back. Pity I'd never considered going to the Charons back then. I knew Pop was one of them so I'd figured they'd have his back, not mine or Ma's. I know how wrong I was now, but back then? I was just a dumb fucking kid, scared of everything around me.

With another deep breath, I forced those thoughts aside and with a smile, turned to face Ma. She didn't look any different than before the disease took hold. Still wore freshly ironed clothes each day and had her hair perfectly styled. But inside her mind, she was rapidly deteriorating. The cold, hard truth of what I needed to do hit me square in the chest as I watched her walk through the room toward me.

The time that I'd been dreading had arrived. Ma now needed more care than I could provide. I couldn't watch her 24/7. She'd proven that three days ago, when she'd wandered off during the night. Thank fuck the front door needed some oil and I'd heard the thing squeaking when she'd opened it. I'd been fast enough to catch her before she got past the gate. But what would have happened if I'd been out? My jaw clenched as my mind churned up scenarios of what might have happened if she'd done something like that while I'd been up north. I'd paid Beth to spend as much time with Ma as I could afford while I'd been away. I still did, but I didn't have the funds to keep it up long-term. Nor could I afford to hire a live-in nurse for her. Guess I'd be calling the local nursing homes to see if I could get her in somewhere. I didn't want to put her in one of those places, but deep down, I realized it was the safest place for her now.

With a quiet sigh, I decided to play along with her tonight. Whenever I'd tried to explain reality to her, she'd get flustered and upset. And in the end, it did nothing but hurt us both. So, it really was just easier to simply pretend to be my father when she got like this. Even though I had no idea how to be the man she was currently remembering.

The Frank Alfonsi who had returned from his time in the USMC was not the same man who had gone in. I'd been fifteen years old when he'd been discharged and had returned home permanently. But that hadn't been the start of his downfall. From what my mother had told me throughout the years, Frank had once been a good man, but with each deployment he lost a little more of himself. Honestly? I had no fucking good memories of my dad. Looking back with an adult's perspective, I could see that he might have left the war, but it never left him. I could only imagine the toll it would take to be constantly fighting your own mind like that. Nearly every night he'd wake screaming, scaring the hell out of me and Ma. It hadn't taken long for him to start drinking. And that had just fueled his rage when he'd thrown a fit. Ma had tried to shield me, tried to tame his fire but it always burned her. He'd lose it and throw a punch. Then, the next morning he'd be mortified by what he'd done, drop down into a black hole of depression and start drinking all over again. It had been a nasty, vicious cycle that had gone on for way too damn long.

Hell, it still shamed me to admit it, but when Pop did kill himself, it had been somewhat of a relief. It would have been nice if he hadn't done it three days prior to my twenty-first birthday, but that was the hand I got dealt. He'd always been glued to news programs and anything about the war on terror, and when, on the 11th of September, 2014, the CIA came out stating that ISIS was so much bigger than anyone had previously guessed, it sent him into a paranoid state. He was sure the USMC would come and pull him back into the war. It was the next morning that I woke to Ma screaming…

I shook the thoughts free and focused on my beautiful mother, who stood before me.

"I'm sure he'll be home any second, Laura. How about I get you a drink? A nice, cold, iced tea, maybe?"

I led her into the kitchen and over to a seat at the table as she began to stammer a response. "Oh. Well, okay. That'll be great. I suppose it's really not that late yet. And, well, boys will be boys."

"That they will, love. Here you go."

I handed her the glass of iced tea and set her pills down in front of her. She frowned a little but thankfully after a few moments, picked them up and swallowed them down. I bit back my sigh of relief. Every now and then she'd argue the need for her medication and it was hell trying to convince her to take the damn things.

Once she was done with her drink and I'd finished my coffee, I followed her lead when she rose up from the seat and took her glass over to the sink. Then she turned to me and her eyes looked clear, giving me a little hope her mind was back in the present. She patted my cheek gently with her palm.

"You're a good boy, Jake. Always have been. When are you going to find a nice girl to settle down with and give me some grandbabies? You don't want to leave it so late, like your father and I did. You want them while you're young, so you can keep up with them."

A flash of Lydia's honey-golden hair and bright green eyes filled my vision for a moment. The sight of her sitting on the bar wearing nothing but my cut was a sight that was burned into my memory. She'd been sexy as fuck and so damn perfect.

"Oh, I know that look! You've met someone haven't you? Oh, my boy, you'll bring her to meet me soon, okay?"

Pain ripped through me at her words. The chances were damn fucking slim that Ma would be around by the time I settled down, and if she was still alive, her mind would no doubt be gone. And it broke my heart that she wouldn't be around to see the grandbabies she'd always wanted so damn badly. Especially considering Lydia had been the only woman to catch my eye in years and I doubted she'd given me a second thought since I'd left New York. Why would she? But Ma didn't need to hear any of that right now. I chose to leave her with the illusion my personal life was looking up.

"Sure, Ma. I'll talk to her about it. C'mon, I'll help you upstairs before I head out."

After I got her settled into bed, I made my way back to the kitchen, where I grabbed a beer before I headed out to sit on the back porch for a bit. Fuck, I was tired. So fucking tired. Sprawling out across the old-school porch swing, I closed my eyes and took a long drink of the cold brew. I had about half an hour before Beth would come to watch over Ma so I could get to the clubhouse, where I was due to man the bar, and I needed a few fucking minutes to myself before I headed down there. I needed to get my head on straight before I had to face everyone and once more act like everything in my world was a-okay, when it was anything but.

Ma reminding me of Lydia sent my thoughts back in time to my trip up north again. Not that my mind needed much encouragement—it seemed whenever I had some downtime that's where my thoughts went. New York had been a whole new world for me. I'd never ventured far from Bridgewater before, certainly never left Texas. Staten Island was different, that's for sure. So many people and cars. But everyone was so friendly. Well, so long as you weren't driving, they were. I shook my head. They sure gave road rage a new meaning up there.

It had been an insane trip. So much had happened in the day and a bit we were up there. But in the end, things turned out well for both us and the Knights. The Riders were no more, and a strong fucking message had been sent to the cartel and the MC world that the Charons and the Satan's Knights were not clubs to be fucked with.

When Mac had first told me my job in the operation was to guard those fucking ledgers I hadn't been happy. Not at all. Turned out it wasn't such a bad gig, though. It meant I got to spend a lot of time with Riggs. He was a tech genius and had used information from the ledgers to track down locations and other shit that enabled us to bring down both the Riders and the cartel. Didn't hurt that Riggs was a real character, too. He was constantly pulling shit on his brothers or trying to get his old lady alone long enough to attempt to put another baby in her.

As I took another pull on my brew, I had to admit, at least to myself, that I missed the man. We'd formed a fast friendship spending so much time together. And then there was Lydia. I definitely missed sassy, beautiful Lydia. I closed my eyes and let the memories flow of our night together. Of how I ate her sweet pussy until she came so hard she was ready to sleep. Not that I let her. Nope, I slid in deep and gave her the ride of her life. Fuck, what I wouldn't give for another night with her sexy ass.

My phone alarm going off brought me back to the present and away from remembering one of the best nights of my life. Fuck. Silencing my phone, I stood and with a huff, rearranged my hard cock before I headed back inside. Tossing my empty beer bottle in the trash, I quietly made my way through the house to check on Ma. Discovering her sound asleep, I headed downstairs and made sure the deadbolts were engaged on both doors so she would be unable to go wandering before Beth turned up. Then I was on my bike and heading over to the clubhouse to do my shift at the bar.

I'd been feeling restless for a while now, long before the trip up north. And it wasn't just because of Ma. The fact I was still nothing but a prospect two years after joining the Charons didn't help. The club seemed happy enough with all that I did for them, but even after all this time I still didn't have my full colors. Mind you, neither did Jazz. It wasn't just me the club seemed to have forgotten about. All the same, it fucking pissed me off that the newer prospects got the same treatment as those of us who'd been there a lot longer.

It was supposed to only take around a year to go from prospect to patched in brother. I had no idea why they'd left the pair of us hanging like they had. I mean, there had been a hell of a lot of shit go down with the club in that time. But still, didn't seem right. And when added to the stress over the situation with my mother, it put me on edge.

That was why later in the night, when I'd finished up my shift behind the bar and was heading out to have a little fun with the boys out by the fire before I headed home, things went south.

"Hey! Bash, need you out front to guard the door."

With a curse, I spun toward the man who'd spoken. I didn't recognize the voice, but if it was a patched in brother, I had to fucking listen and obey. When I saw it was not only a prospect, but a new one, I narrowed my eyes. Who did this fucking bastard think he was?

"I've done my work for the night, how about you go do yours, yeah?"

He had one of the club whores pressed up against a wall and clearly had plans for her, but fuck him. I wasn't going to take shit from a newbie prospect and take over his job so he could ball a fucking club whore.

Releasing her, he turned on me. "What the fuck is your problem? You're a prospect, just like me. Doesn't matter which of us is on the front door. And we all know you won't be making use of the girls so what gives?"

A prospect like him. His words rang in my ears like a fucking church bell. Then something snapped and with a growl, I lunged at the fucker. Leading with a fist, it cracked against his jaw, snapping his head to the side before he could react.

"I ain't like you. I've been here two fucking years and have earned my fucking place. Unlike you, I've never fucking slacked off. I was on the bar tonight, just finished my shift, so now I'm gonna enjoy my fucking down time, not do your fucking job for you so you can get your dick wet."

He recovered from my blow and with a curse, threw one back at me. I knocked it aside as I slammed my other fist into his gut.

"Two years? What did you do to make 'em hold off on your patch like that?"

My vision went red because wasn't that the question of the day. Barely aware of my movements, I kept throwing punches and kicks as he hurled them back. He landed some good shots, but I didn't feel a thing. Rage, pure and lethal, flowed through me.

"Enough!"

Keys' voice echoed around the room as a thick arm went around my neck and hauled me back.

"C'mon, buddy. Settle down."

Recognizing Keg's voice, I stopped struggling and closed my eyes. After a couple deep breaths, my body relaxed and he loosened his hold.

"We good?"

"Yeah. I'm calm."

I opened my eyes to look for the prospect who had started it all. He was standing on the other side of the room, pressing a towel to his nose that was bleeding like a fountain. He was glaring at me so I glared right back. Fucking prick.

Keys pointed to the other guy. "You. Get your ass in the kitchen and let my woman take a look at you. Try anything with her and you'll be a dead man. Bank, go with 'em."

Donna was a nurse and was well-practiced at patching up Charons. I watched as Bank all but dragged the prospect down the hall before Keys turned to me.

"You—"

Arrow cut him off. "You go with the others to your woman, I'll take care of Bash."

Not giving Keys time to argue, Arrow gave me a nod then turned and headed toward the offices. Pulling free from Keg's hold on me, I followed. The clubhouse was unnaturally silent and I wondered if I was about to be shown the door. Permanently. And that got me wondering if that wouldn't be such a bad thing.

He unlocked a door and held it open for me to enter before he closed it and moved past me to lean against the desk that sat in the center of the space.

"Sit your ass down, boy."

Suddenly feeling tired as hell, I allowed my body to crumple onto the couch. I went to rub a palm over my face but the moment I made contact, it hurt like hell so I dropped my hand back down.

"Yeah, that shit's gonna hurt for a while. Of course, not as much as young Brett's gonna be feeling it. What'd he do?"

"Nothing. It was nothing."

"That's a load of bullshit and we both know it. Don't make me waste time by tracking down Keys and getting him to bring up the feed from the cameras."

Fucking Keys. Felt like he had every inch of the whole damn town wired some days.

Over everything and wanting to get this shit over with, with a growl, I started talking.

"It'd been a long fucking day before I even got here. Then just as I'd finished my shift at the bar and was heading out to the fire for a couple drinks of my own with the others, he tried to order me to take his place out front. All so he could ball a fucking club whore."

Arrow's gaze narrowed for a minute as he watched me. I cleared my throat and squirmed some as the silence dragged on. I just wanted this shit over with already so I could go home and end this fucking day.

"While that was a pansy-ass move for him to pull, it's not something that would normally send you into a rage like that. If Keg hadn't pulled you off him, do you think you would have stopped any time soon?"

A sudden wave of shame filled me. We both knew the answer to that. I wouldn't have. I would have killed Brett if we hadn't been stopped. I hung my head, shaking it no to answer him.

"Bash, this ain't like you. Normally? A prospect pulls shit like this, they'd be shown the door and not welcome back, but you're not really a standard prospect—"

He stopped talking when I glared up at him, some of my earlier rage returning.

"Starting to think all I'll ever be 'round here is a fucking prospect."

He nodded, his expression dead serious. "It's been too long. We all know it. You've earned your colors. Scout was planning on taking it to a vote once this shit with Sabella got dealt with. But that's just a formality, we all know you'll get voted in." He held my gaze for a few moments before continuing. "The fact you don't look happy about that makes me think this is about something else. You've been on edge for a while now and I'd assumed it was about the lack of a back patch on your cut, but now I'm thinking otherwise. The time has come for you to quit hiding shit and fucking tell me what's got you hurting like you are."

I held his gaze as my thoughts tripped over themselves. There was so much, and did he really want to know? Did I want him to know?

Arrow grabbed a chair, and putting it on the floor in front of me, straddled it backwards, resting his arms on the top of the back of the thing and staring me straight in the eye.

"Is it your ma?"

My fucking eyes stung as Arrow hit the nail on the head first go. What the fuck? Was the man psychic? Sucking in a breath I rubbed my eyes, forcing the moisture away before Arrow saw it.

"Is it another tumor?"

I shook my head. "No tumor. At least, not that we know about. Fuck, I guess it could be another one that's causing it. She was diagnosed with early onset Alzheimer's a while back."

"Ah, fuck, man. Why didn't you tell us? We wouldn't have sent you up north if we'd known."

That left me wincing. I wouldn't have met Lydia, wouldn't have had my night with her if they'd known.

Arrow chuckled darkly. "Although, you did enjoy your time up there, didn't you? Maybe the break away was just what you needed. Either way, if we'd known, we would have given you time off from doing club jobs. You need to spend all the time you can with your ma before it's too late."

With a sad smile I shook my head. "It's already too late half the time. Guess I look just like my old man did when he was younger. I spend more time pretending to be my pop than I do being myself at this point."

"She still living at home?"

I nodded. "Yeah. I made some calls today to try to get her into a home but there's fucking waiting lists everywhere."

"What made you call today?"

I huffed at him with a shake of my head. "You came by your name honestly, didn't you?"

He shrugged a shoulder. "Straight as an arrow, straight to the heart of the problem. Gets the job done."

I shook my head again. "She wandered off a few nights back. The front door on our place needed oil in a bad way so I heard it open. Managed to catch her before she got past the front gate. But it was an eye opener."

Silence filled the room and I started rubbing at my throbbing jaw. I'd gotten in more hits than Brett, but he did manage to get a couple in that I'd be feeling for the next day or so.

"You good to ride home, or you want a lift?"

"I'll be fine on my bike."

He gave me a nod. "Take the rest of the week off. Ten am Saturday you'll be back here. We're gonna have a sit down and get shit sorted out. Now, get outta here and go home. Might wanna put some ice on your jaw and that eye."

He stood and shoved the chair back to where it had been as I rose and groaned at the ache in my ribs that started up with my movement. Fuck, I was gonna be feeling that shit in the morning. Arrow gave me a slap to the shoulder as I passed him and headed out to the main room. Things had returned to the usual noisy state that the clubhouse was in this late at night and I managed to slip out the front door without gaining too much attention.

Chapter 5

The next morning I'd managed to keep my head down and avoid Ma as I got ready for work and headed out. Beth had cocked an eyebrow at my busted-up face but hadn't said a word.

The boys on the construction site didn't say a thing about it, but I knew they wouldn't. It was far from the first time one of our crew had rocked up looking worse for wear. Thankfully the day passed quickly and before I knew it, I was back home bidding Beth farewell and closing the door behind her.

"You gonna tell me who did that to your face?"

Closing my eyes, I took a deep breath before I reopened my lids and turned to face my mother. I wasn't sure if she thought I was me or my old man yet, so I wasn't sure what the fuck to tell her. She stood a few feet from me with her arms crossed over her chest. Her jaw was a hard line and the glint in her eyes had me thinking she was having a good day and knew who I was.

"It's nothing, Ma. Had a bit of a disagreement with one of the boys down the clubhouse last night."

Her gaze narrowed as it ran over me, I could feel her cataloging all my injuries with her mom radar.

"The clubhouse, huh? And where was Scout when this was happening?"

I frowned. The way she said his name had my own radar going. Sure, she'd have known he was the president from when my pops had been in the club, but Ma never hung around the club like some of the other old ladies. She didn't even speak with him at Pop's funeral, so why was she now dropping his name like they were friends?

"I believe he was home with his woman and kids. His son is only a few months old so he doesn't do the late night stuff too often these days."

She came up to me and took my chin between her thumb and finger, shifting my face to get a good look at the bruising and swelling along my jaw, cheekbone and eye.

"Would it make you feel better if I told you the other guy looks a lot worse than me?"

She actually growled a little, which made me smile. I'd missed my mother so much. It had been hard having her physically close, yet mentally so far away.

"No, it would not. You're not a brawler, Jake. What the hell got into you? And I'll be talking to Scout. He promised me!"

I gently removed her hand from where she was adding a bruise to my chin.

"Ma, calm down. I ain't hurt that bad. It's nothing that won't heal in a couple of days. What do you mean, Scout promised you?"

She clenched her jaw before she spun on her heel and headed away from me. I followed her, not only wanting an answer to my question but I also didn't want to waste a moment of this time that she was lucid and knew who I was.

She went to the kitchen and poured two glasses of iced tea before she sat at the table, sliding a glass over to me when I followed her lead and sat opposite her.

"About two years ago, just before my surgery, I went to Scout to ask him a favor. You see, not only were they in that club together, but Scout was in the Marines with your father as well. They served together for a time. So, I went to him and asked that he watch over you." She paused with a wince and took a drink before she continued in a hushed voice. "I wasn't sure I'd survive the surgery."

With my heart aching, I thought back to that time when Scout and Bulldog had first approached me, inviting me to come to the clubhouse for a beer. I'd been reeling over Ma's upcoming surgery, throwing myself into work and not much else. In my attempts to avoid my old man at all times, I'd never considered the Charons as a viable option for me until then. But honestly? The club had been a nice change of pace. A place I could really relax and let go. I could see why my pop spent so much time there. Pretty much every man there had some kind of demon chasing him, and they'd not busted my balls over the fact I was keeping quiet about what mine was. They hadn't wanted to get in my head and work me out which suited me just fine.

It had been a few months later, after Ma had her surgery and pulled through, that Scout had invited me to become a prospect. I'd jumped at the chance, feeling like I'd found where I fit in the world. Now I started to wonder how much of that invite was out of obligation to his promise to his former Charon and USMC brother's widow, and nothing to do with me.

"I hadn't been sure encouraging you into that life was a good idea, but I could see you getting lost. Working all the damn time and fussing after me when you weren't. You needed more in your life, son. You needed something that would make you smile and it seemed like the Charon MC gave you that. At least it did. Now I can't remember the last time I saw you smile." She frowned with a sigh. "Of course, that could be due to me not remembering, rather than you not smiling. I'm sorry you're getting saddled with me being sick again. You're young. You should be out there riding free and having fun. Not here, probably worried every time you see me if I'll still remember who you are."

Her voice cut out on a sob and my fucking eyes stung with emotion. Under the illness, she knew more than I'd thought she would. I reached out and wrapped a hand around hers.

"Ma, I'd do anything for you. You need me, I'm here. Always."

She brushed her tears away with her free hand. "Such a charmer. Were you telling me the truth the other day? About having a woman?"

After giving her hand a pat, I pulled mine back and took a drink of the cold iced tea. "I did meet a woman, while I was up in New York. But I'm not sure when I'll be able to see her again."

She gave me a sad smile that had me worried about where she was heading with this conversation.

"Maybe a fresh start in a new place would do you good. Maybe it's time I moved into a home and let you spread your wings some."

My eyes widened in shock. "Ma, I'd never shove you into a home then move clear halfway across the country."

She chuckled. "I know you'd come visit me as often as you could. And sadly, I don't know how much longer my mind is going to give me. No use in you being held down by me when I don't know who you are anymore."

Her voice hitched at the end again and tears now streamed down her cheeks. I hated this. All of it. The fucking disease that was stealing so much from us both. The fact neither of us had control over our lives. My heart ached. We were both stuck in a cycle of merely surviving, neither of us really living our lives.

"Ah, Ma. Come here."

I stood and pulled her up from her chair, tugging her in against my chest as I wrapped my arms around the woman who'd loved me with her whole heart since before I'd been born. As her tears soaked my shirt, I found I couldn't blink fast enough to stop my own from falling. Somewhere deep inside, I knew this was going to be one of the last times I had with my Ma fully lucid, and it fucking shattered me. The very thought of losing the one constant I'd always had in my life was more than I could process.

"I love you, Ma, and I'd never abandon you, no matter what."

Her grip on me tightened and we just stood there for a long time, before she pulled back, patted my chest with her palm and headed out of the kitchen toward her room. I grabbed a beer and moved out to the back porch. Sitting in the swing and rocking myself, I let my thoughts wander as I watched the sun head toward the horizon.

No matter what Ma said, I couldn't leave Bridgewater while she was still here, but her suggestion of a fresh start had me thinking. I'd enjoyed Staten Island. And not just because of Lydia. It was always busy. People and cars everywhere. There was always something happening. People busy getting shit done. And the food. Damn. Nothing quite like New York pizza and cannoli. My stomach let out a grumble in memory of the delicious little cream-filled delights that Riggs had introduced me to. We'd been on our way to the bank when Riggs declared we had to stop at Alfonso's Pastry Shop. I'd thought he was fucking nuts until I got to eat those cannoli. Then I'd understood his insistence on stopping for them.

Before I realized what I was doing, I had my phone out and had hit dial on Riggs' number.

"Well, if it isn't the Ron Jeremy of the twenty-first century," he greeted, making sure to toss in a dig about walking in on me and Lydia. "What's up, my man?"

"Not a whole helluva lot."

Suddenly not sure what the fuck to say, I took a swig of my beer.

"You doing okay down there in cowboy country, Moses?"

There was that utterly ridiculous name again, but I couldn't muster the energy to rip into him for using it. I looked out over the backyard and into the field that was behind our place. Not a living thing for as far as the eye could see. So fucking isolated.

"It's so fucking quiet down here."

"Yeah. You know, I don't know if I told you, but I used to live in Texas. Come to think of it, I probably didn't. My last name is Montgomery."

Everyone in Texas knew about the Montgomerys. They owned one of the largest oil operations in the country.

"Anyway, I hightailed it out of there as soon as I could. Followed Bones up here and made a life for myself. I'm not sure I'd know what to do with all that fucking silence anymore."

That made me grin. "Well, try wrapping it up on occasion and you wouldn't have so many kids running around making so much noise."

His deep laugh rumbled down the line. "Fuck that. The way I see it, I got another two or three cubs to make before Kitten either castrates me or forces me to get a vasectomy. But I wasn't just referring to the kids. I don't think I could fall asleep at night without hearing the occasional car speed down the street or my neighbors fighting."

I nodded, even though he couldn't see me. "Staten Island sure was different from here. So many cars and people everywhere. All the time. Day and night. It was nice. It's like you're never alone."

"Big cities can be lonely as fuck too, man. Before Kitten, all I had was Bones. He was already a patched member and I was still a prospect, which meant he was off in the wild and I was fucking scrubbing floors. Anyway, it was lonely and at times boring as fuck. But I don't gotta tell you how that goes, do I?"

"Considering I've been a prospect for nearly two fucking years now, I know how it goes, all right. I've worked my ass off for the Charons in that time. Never once slacked off. Hell, I even took a fucking bullet on one job. But I'm still without my full colors."

"Two fucking years? Shit. Things really do move slowly down there. You speak to Scout about it?"

"Nah, Arrow talked to me last night, after I beat the shit out of a new prospect. Told me they've been meaning to vote on it but shit keeps going down and distracting the club."

"Wait, you beat the shit outta another prospect and you didn't get shown the door? What the fuck happened, Moses? You don't strike me as a hothead. They give you that road name because you bash in skulls?"

I scoffed a laugh. "Wanna know the truth behind my road name?"

I suspected I'd regret letting Riggs know this one, but it was easier to talk about than the reason behind me beating on Brett.

"Sure, man. Origin stories are always good. Should I get some popcorn?"

That made me scoff again. "When I first joined the club, I wasn't used to being surrounded by so many women all the time and I'd get nervous as hell when I was around them. Even the old ladies. Mac was teasing me one night about being bashful around his old lady, Bulldog overheard it and declared my new name was Bash. Although, after last night, maybe I've earned it for a different reason."

"What happened?"

Riggs wasn't laughing at my story. In fact, his voice had lost all the levity it normally contained. Like he knew I was on the edge. I took another swig of beer before I answered him.

"I'd just finished my stint behind the bar and was heading out to the yard for a few drinks before I came home, when a newer recruit was in the process of getting up the skirt of one of the club whores and tried to pass off his shift at guarding the front door to me, 'cause I was just a prospect like him. Fuck. I just saw red. I've never had that happen before. Keg pulled me off him before I killed him. Fuck. I can't believe I lost it like that, to be honest."

"We all got our breaking point, man. Looks like this fucker found yours."

"I guess. Arrow pulled me aside and grilled me. When he found out about my ma, he gave me the week off duties. Supposed to be going in Saturday to sit down with Scout."

"You worried they're going to show you the door?"

"I know I should be. I mean, two years I've given the Charons, but right now, with Ma like she is… I don't know. I just… Fuck. I just can't muster up the energy to give a shit if I'm in or out. You feel me?"

"Those are some serious words, man," he said. "How is your ma doing these days?"

"She's bad. I mean tonight she's been good. With it enough to give me a dressing down over getting in a fight. But those moments where she knows who the fuck I am are getting further and further apart."

I stopped to take another swig of beer, not really sure what else I could say.

"I'm gonna tell you something someone told me a long time ago. Take the detour. Sometimes the path we thought we were meant to travel, ain't the right one. It doesn't mean we don't get where we're supposed to be and should you feel the need to make a right instead of a left, do it. Don't fucking hesitate. Maybe you need a change of scenery or a pretty little bartender to lick your wounds."

"Thanks, Riggs. To be honest, I've been thinking a change of pace might be a good thing. But I gotta settle things with Ma first."

"Family first. Always. I gotta get my ass in gear. Remember what I said, and if you ever wanna move north, let me know and I'll talk to Wolf. Bet Lydia wouldn't mind having Ron Jeremy back in town. Maybe then she'll quit bitching and moping around here."

With that parting shot, he hung up, leaving me speechless and back to remembering the sassy, sexy woman I'd had just one night with. A woman who instantly made the idea of moving to New York a whole lot more appealing.

With five minutes to spare, I pulled my bike up into the lot in front of the clubhouse. It had felt strange not coming in for the past few days, that's for sure. Although, I'd made the most of spending more time with Ma. Even when I'd had to pretend to be my old man, or explain to her I was her son when she didn't remember either me or my pop, it was still nice just to be near her. As much as I didn't like it, I knew time was not on our side and I wouldn't have her for much longer.

This early on a Saturday, the clubhouse was fairly quiet with only a few men hanging around the main rooms. I made fast work of heading back to Scout's office and knocked on the open door before entering.

Scout looked up. "Bash, come on in."

Unsure of how things were going to go, I closed the door behind me before moving to sit in one of the chairs in front of his desk. With a sigh, Scout opened a drawer and pulled a folder out, placing it in front of me but keeping his palm on the thing, preventing me from seeing what it was for the moment.

"I wish you'd come to me earlier, Bash. Could've had your ma settled in somewhere sooner."

He released the folder and gave me a nod to open it. Flipping the cover over, I did a double-take at what it contained.

"How the fuck did you get her a room? I was told we'd be waiting at least four months."

"We got a lot of pull in this town. Over the years we've helped a lot of folks out of tight situations. Favors are owed and I collected on one. You're not alone, Jake. You're a member of this club, and that means your family comes under my protection and care. I'm sorry I haven't spent more time with you lately. If I'd been doing my fucking job I would have known you were struggling. For that I apologize." He paused to run his hand through his hair. "It seems lately, the bullshit keeps flying our way faster than we can shovel it away. But that ain't no excuse. A lot of things have been left to slide, but we're gonna fix that shit. We'll get your ma settled in up at Oakford Home on Monday, then Friday night at church we'll put the vote through and get your top rocker sorted. We all know you earned the right to wear it a long fucking time ago. You and Jazz both have."

He stopped talking until I shifted my gaze from the Oakford Home agreement on the desk to meet his gaze. I was in a state of shock and awe. I hadn't even considered asking Scout about whether he held any sway with the home. I mean, this was a motorcycle club and that was an old folks' home.

"You're being awful damn quiet. What's going on in that head of yours?"

"I'm in shock, still trying to process what just happened. I half expected to come in today and be told I was out for good after that fight with Brett. But instead you've given me the solution I'd been praying for but hadn't been expecting."

He gave me a solemn nod. "It's true we don't normally accept brawling like that from hangarounds or prospects, but as I said, you should have had a full patch a long time ago. I can understand why you snapped. You're under a shit-ton of pressure right now and Brett pushed his responsibilities onto you just so he could chase the skirt of a club whore. Dare say no matter who he'd tried that shit on, it would have ended with him nursing a sore jaw. He's out, by the way."

That had me sitting straighter. "He's not gonna come gunning for me now, is he?"

I knew admitting that fear made me sound like a wuss, but with everything else I had going on, having to worry about Brett was the last thing I needed.

"I doubt it. But we're keeping an eye on him for the next few weeks, just in case. He'd already been warned about his lack of commitment to the club before the other night. He knows it wasn't the fight so much as the fact he wanted to fuck one of the whores more than he wanted to pull his weight that got him booted. If you hear from him or see him hanging around at all, you let us know and we'll deal with it."

I relaxed back into the chair, scrubbing a hand over my face, trying to wrap my head around everything Scout had told me just now, and trying to work out how to ask about what Ma had told me earlier in the week.

"Ma was having a good day Thursday. Convenient for her since it meant she got to rip me a new one over brawling and coming home beat up."

Scout scoffed a chuckle. "Guessing telling her the other guy looked worse didn't help your cause?"

"Not one bit. Then she asked me where you were when it went down. Told me how she asked you to look out for me. Got me wondering if that was the only reason you asked me to prospect in was as a favor to a fallen club and Marine brother."

With a wince, Scout stood and silently went over to gather a bottle of whiskey and two glasses from a shelf before returning and pouring each of us a drink.

"Yeah, the reason you were first approached was due to your ma asking a favor of me. A favor I agreed to, due to the fact I'd known your old man as a Marine and a club brother. Asking you to join the Charons was never part of what I promised your ma. She just wanted me to keep my eye on you, make sure you were doing okay. Especially if her surgery didn't go well."

He paused to take a mouthful from his drink, so I followed his lead, enjoying the burn of the whiskey as I waited for him to continue.

"I didn't ask you to come hang out here because of that favor. I could have easily kept my word without involving the club, but after that first night we chatted, I thought you could use the support the Charons would give you. Thought you'd enjoy it here. You've certainly earned the right to call yourself a Charon. Guess the question is, do you still want it?"

I swirled the amber liquid in the glass before I tossed the rest of it down my throat, setting a fire flaring from my mouth down to my belly in the process. Scout had the good stuff hidden away here in his office.

"Honestly? I barely know which way is up lately, let alone what I fucking want for the future."

He gave me another of his head tilts. "Well, let's leave it for now. We'll get your ma settled into Oakford, then you let me know before church at the end of the week what you want to do. Sound fair?"

"Sounds good."

Scout polished off the last of his drink before tapping the empty glass on the desk.

"Well, I guess you'd best get to packing. Give me a call if you need help and switch out your bike for one of the club's cages for the weekend so you can get shit done."

I set my glass next to his. "Thanks. I'll keep my bike for now, but I'll drop in Sunday night and switch rides. I doubt she'll want to take much with her, so I should be all right to handle it. It's going to be tough enough trying to keep her calm with all the new faces at the home, don't want to add more than is necessary."

"Fair enough. But the offer stands. I'm serious, Jake. You are not alone. We're all here and we've got your back. All you gotta do is reach out and accept it."

Before I could respond, my phone rang in my pocket. Standing up, I fished it out to see who was calling and when I saw it was Beth the blood left my head so fast a wave of dizziness hit me that had nothing to do with the high-priced whiskey I'd just put away.

Scout growled, "What the fuck?"

In the few moments it took me to hit answer, Scout was standing in front of me. I was staring straight into his hard, blue eyes when I spoke into my phone.

"Hey, Beth, Ma okay?"

"Oh, honey, I'm so sorry. She was feeling tired earlier so laid down for a nap before lunch. I just went to wake her but I couldn't. I'm truly sorry, Jake—"

The phone slipped from my hand, and Scout caught it before it hit the floor. He lifted it to his ear and spoke but I heard none of it. I stood frozen, unable to move, unable to process what had just happened. I was vaguely aware there were tears running down my face, but in that moment, I didn't give a fuck that Scout was witnessing me cry.

My mother was gone.

Just when I was starting to get shit sorted out for her.

Life was so fucking unfair.

Chapter 6

Three days later, I stood beside Ma's grave. Alone. The funeral had been a short, graveside thing and with the exception of Beth, it had been attended solely by Charons. The old ladies had arranged a wake back at the clubhouse, but I wasn't ready to leave yet. Leaving would make it all the more final. I took in the headstone, the weather-worn text of my father's final resting place alongside the glossy, fresh engraving on my mother's side.

For the most part, I was still numb. Inside and out. I was officially an orphan. Didn't matter that I was a grown man. At twenty-five years old, I felt like I was nothing more than a child as I stood there praying this was all nothing but a nightmare. That I'd wake up and have both my parents back, both in perfect mental health. Fuck, I'd take just one of them back. I didn't want to be alone.

Clearing my throat and blinking away more tears, I let my gaze run over the flowers that covered the coffin, the single, large, bright yellow sunflower standing out. Scout's daughter, Ariel, had added it. That little girl was nothing short of inspiring. Put me to shame, really. She was just five years old and had already been forced to bury her own mother. We hadn't known which of those fuckers out in that cult had been her father, but we'd killed every one of them who'd ever raped her mother, so she was an orphan too. But she wasn't alone. Scout and Marie had adopted her and she had the entire Charon MC at her back. Little mite knew it, too. Over the months since we'd rescued her, she'd grown stronger and more confident. Especially once she had a little brother to protect. She didn't let her past hold her down. Like I said, the kid was an inspiration.

I knew I had the club at my back, too. As evidenced by the wake that was currently going on back at the clubhouse, waiting for me. But was I strong enough to put my past behind me like Ariel had?

"C'mon, son. Let's head to the clubhouse."

Scout gripped my shoulder, giving it a squeeze. Letting me know that I wasn't really alone. Like Ariel, I had the Charon MC to back me up. But was that going to be enough? Scout had told me my back patch was mine as soon as I was ready to accept it, but was being a patched in member of the Charon MC going to be enough? Riggs' voice filled my mind, telling me to take the damn detour already, which was followed by flashes of Lydia's sexy smirk as I turned and followed Scout back to our bikes. Take the detour. What could it hurt? I had nothing else to lose, but I didn't want to make any big decisions so close to burying Ma. I'd give it another few days at least, before I made any final decision about my future.

Another two days had passed me by in a blur and I was still unsure on whether I should act on Riggs' advice and take the detour, or if I should just stay here with what I knew. If I wasn't at the building site, I was here at the clubhouse working, or hiding out with a beer. I'd avoided going back home. Every inch of that old house reminded me of what I'd lost. The silence there was suffocating, so I stayed at the clubhouse. It was still lonely as fuck, but at least I wasn't swamped with memories when I saw every little thing that reminded me of happier times with my ma.

The club whores were trying their best to entice me into letting them cheer me up but I couldn't go there. Couldn't even think of touching a woman who wasn't Lydia. It was fucked up. Not only was she on the other side of the damn country, but we'd only shared one night together and I was all hung up on her like a lovesick pup.

That's how I came to be sitting on the edge of the bed in my room here at the clubhouse. Avoiding everyone's good intentions as I drank a beer and stared out the window at the star-studded night sky while the noise from downstairs floated up through the floor. Lost in my numbness, I didn't even check who was calling when my phone started ringing before I answered it.

"Hey."

"Hey, man, heard about your ma and wanted to pass on my condolences."

"Thanks, Riggs."

"How you holding up?"

I didn't answer. Mainly because I had no fucking clue what to say.

"Shit, man, you got everyone worried about you."

That caught my attention and pulled away a little of the fog clouding my mind. "Whatcha mean by everyone? And worried about what?"

"What the fuck do you think I mean? Spoke with Arrow, told me you got offered your patch and turned it down. That true?"

Closing my eyes on a sigh I stretched out my neck before responding. MC brothers were worse than a pack of schoolgirls when it came to gossip.

"I didn't turn it down so much as I haven't accepted it. Been a little busy to give it the thought it deserves."

"Don't bullshit me, Moses. You forget all you told me while you were up here? Let me see if I can take a guess at where you're at. You haven't been back to your house since you lost your ma. You're crashing at the clubhouse, but avoiding everybody and everything as much as you can. You still working or have you abandoned that too?"

Bastard saw too much. "I'm still working."

My words were little more than a growl. I didn't like he'd pinned me so well.

"Last time we spoke, you mentioned wanting a fresh start. Nothing is holding you down there now, why not come up here for a while? Nothing has to be forever, man."

I drained the last of my beer. He was right, dammit. I'd been feeling like I was stuck in survival mode before Ma passed, now she was gone I was still just going through the motions. Not living. Just breathing.

Something had to give. *Take the detour.*

"Your ma would want you to live, to find some fucking joy in life. For fuck's sake she'd want you to find your heart. Dammit, I'm starting to sound like Parrish."

I had no clue what to say to that. I'd heard Parrish go on about finding your heart when I'd been up in New York. Was Lydia my heart? Was that why I couldn't quit thinking about her, even when everything else in my life had ground to a halt? A blast of anger fired through me that Riggs had me over-thinking everything so damn much when I just wanted to be left the fuck alone. Who the fuck did Riggs think he was?

"You fucking done psychoanalyzing me?"

"You ready to man the fuck up and buy a plane ticket yet? Take the motherfucking detour already." He paused and a sigh carried over the line. "Look, I didn't call to bust your balls. Tonight, at church, I brought up your situation and Wolf took a vote. Everyone agreed you could prospect here if you choose. Of course, Wolf would talk to Scout about it too, but if that's what you wanted, it could be done. It's your choice, man. Why not take some time, a couple of weeks away from everything that reminds you of what you've lost?"

I was done with talking with Riggs. Bastard was making me fucking think when I didn't want to.

"Yeah, whatever. Look, I'll think about it, okay?"

"Right, well let me know when you want a pick up from the airport."

He hung up and I reached over to put my phone and the empty bottle on the bedside table before I flopped back on the bed.

Fuck my life. I didn't want to make any kind of decision. I was back to being that fucking little kid hoping to wake up and the nightmare to be over. I rubbed at my eyes as they stung with emotion at the thought of living the rest of my fucking life without my mother in it.

When my phone chimed with a message, I nearly ignored it, not wanting to see whatever Riggs was pulling now. But within minutes, my curiosity got the better of me and I snatched up the device. It was a video message. However, it wasn't from Riggs but an unknown number. Clicking into the message, my breath caught when an up-close image of Lydia's chest filled the screen, her low cut top revealing the slight swell of her tits, making my mouth water. The camera moved and focused on her face. Her pouty lips and sad eyes drew me in just like they had every time I'd seen her.

"Hey, cowboy. Heard about your mom I just wanted to tell you how sorry I am and let you know I'm thinking about you. I wish we lived closer so I could give you a hug. Anyway, I hope you're okay."

With that she blew me a kiss and the message ended.

Fuck me, but I missed her.

Suddenly my decision became clear. Like somehow, between Riggs and Lydia, a switch had been flipped within me and I knew exactly what I needed to do.

Where I needed to go.

Who I needed to see.

Take the motherfucking detour.

Opening up Google on my phone, I looked up plane tickets and booked the next available, which was unfortunately not until the morning. I was done sitting around here, lost in memories. Riggs had been right. Ma wouldn't want me to just fade into oblivion now she'd gone. She'd want me to live my life, have the grandbabies she always wanted me to give her. Even if she'd never meet them.

I then shot a text off to Riggs.

See you at Newark at 10:30am tomorrow

Within seconds I got one back.

About damn time. C U soon.

With a smile, I set about shoving the few things I'd brought to the clubhouse in a bag. I'd head home and pack up enough for a few weeks. I still wasn't sure if permanently moving to New York was what I should do, but a few weeks up there to decide wasn't going to hurt anything. If, after a few weeks I decided to stay up north, I'd come back, hand my cut in to Scout and get the house dealt with, then ship the rest of my stuff up there before flying back myself.

For the first time in months, I had a solid plan and damn, it felt good. I actually felt lighter on my feet as I made my way downstairs to the main floor to start searching for one of the club officers. I found Arrow out by the fire pit and he rose an eyebrow at the bag over my shoulder as I approached.

"Made your decision then?"

"Yep. Gonna fly out in the morning, head north for a bit. See how I like hanging out with the Knights. I'll be back in a couple weeks, either to pack up and move for good or to settle back in here. Is that going to be okay? Or do you want my cut now?"

Arrow gave my shoulder a squeeze. "Keep your cut, Bash. You come see us in a couple weeks when you get back and feel free to call any one of us if you need anything at all. You understand?"

While trying really fucking hard to not get emotional, I gave him a nod. "Of course."

"Right, well, it's your last night here so let's knock a few drinks back to celebrate. Go drop your bag someplace and get your ass back out here."

I was going to miss the men and women of the Charon MC, but I had a good feeling about this detour and couldn't wait to see where it was going to take me.

To Be Continued…

Bash is headed to New York and Khloe is handing over the reins to Janine Bosco.
Read his full-length novel, Shifting Gears and find out what happens when he crosses paths with the Satan's Knights MC.

Turn the page for a sneak peek at Shifting Gears

Blurb:

They're called one-night stands for a reason. If you're lucky, there's a lot of mind-blowing sex and then you never have to see or speak to the person again. It's fun and uncomplicated. In my case, Bash hightailed it to the airport the next morning so I definitely never expected to run into the former prospect for the Charon MC again. But when his mother passed, he dragged his pipes all the way from Texas to New York, and now he's crashing at the Satan's Knights clubhouse. Which also happens to be where I work and the scene of our one-night crime. If I thought forgetting the orgasm champ was hard before, it just became damn impossible.

Grief can shake a man, make him question his whole damn life and have him taking chances he never thought he'd take. Chances like moving to Staten Island, New York. Chances like prospecting for a new club. Chances like being around a certain fiery bartender who has been in my head since we shared one incredible night. Even though I should be completely focused on earning my colors, there's a part of me that wants to chance chasing Lydia Gallo for more than one night. I want to break down her walls and uncover every one of her secrets...patch be damned.

Shifting Gears
By Janine Infante Bosco

Prologue

Lydia

"Shit," I hiss as the glass tumbles out of my hand and crashes to the floor, shattering into a million tiny pieces. Another fine mess I'll have to clean before I go home. Dead on my feet, I mutter a curse and drop to my knees, carefully avoiding the shards of glass.

When I first took the job at Big Nose Kate's I thought it would be a piece of cake. Okay, so I wasn't actually licensed bartender, big deal. I made a mean margarita and I could pop the top off a long neck with the bottom of a lighter. I was totally qualified for the job. Or so I thought. I had no idea I would be working for the Satan's Knights motorcycle club. I mean, an Italian woman by the name of Maria Bianci interviewed me and there wasn't a stitch of leather to be found on that woman. She was all class. Then I met her son-in-law, the actual owner of the bar. Riggs or Tiger, depending on his mood. He was most definitely a biker. He had the vest, the rank, and the gunshot wounds to prove it. As intimidating as my new boss was, he was also a real ball buster who lived to crack jokes and impregnate his girl. He didn't care that I wasn't licensed, and I soon learned the bar was more of a front for their clubhouse. It was open to the public, but I mostly served the club and they drank the hard stuff. As long as I kept their glasses full, I was golden.

It wasn't until a couple of days ago that I really started to wonder if I had lost my fucking mind by taking the job. The Satan's Knights were in a heap of trouble and housing a club from out of town. The former president of the club, Jack Parrish, was due to surrender to authorities when his wife was injured in a car accident. They soon discovered the Sinaloa Cartel had been responsible for Reina's accident and the new president, Wolf, also Maria's man, put the entire club on lockdown. I didn't know what that meant and to be fair, I didn't think it had anything to do with me. I was just the girl behind the bar getting everyone wasted. What the fuck did I care about some drug lords? The Knights, the Charons, Moe, Larry, and Curly…they were all buzzed. A job well done on my part if you ask me.

I didn't realize how serious things were until Wolf told me I couldn't leave, that no one was going anywhere until he was a hundred percent certain it was safe. At first, I laughed in his face, annihilating any chance of becoming an employee of the month. In my defense, I was on the heels of a thirteen-hour shift and I was sure the big beast of a man was pulling my chain. The laughter quickly died on my lips when he slid the deadbolt into place and ordered me back behind the bar. Instantly, the memories of a life I escaped resurfaced, and I was no longer the quirky bartender trying to get by. Instead, I was the terrorized woman who stood in her husband's shadows. A woman who knew nothing but fear, torment, and abuse. The next drink I poured was for myself and I made it a double. I reminded myself that I was safe and hundreds of miles away from the pain and suffering. Nothing and no one would ever touch me. I spent the last two years making sure of it, of making sure there were no traces of that life to be found. What was happening here, had nothing to do with me. I was just a victim of circumstance in this situation.

In the days that followed things were intense, and I was suddenly grateful to the women of the club who provided me with clean clothes on the daily and somehow managed to keep my mind from wandering to that dark forbidden place. The men were pulled in different directions and came and went as duty called. They were working closely with the other club and at one point I found myself curiously staring at the Charon left in charge of guarding a bunch of books. He went by the name of Bash and I told myself I was only intrigued by the literature that held his attention and not his soulful blue eyes that kept mine. He was quiet and expressionless but there was an intensity to him that made him just as lethal as the rest of the bunch. Solitude wasn't a choice, it was a means of survival for me, so it was crazy and completely out of character for me to be interested in anyone. Especially a man. But there was something about him. Something that called to a part of me I thought was buried.

Earlier today the Knights and the Charons neutralized the threat and the ban to leave the bar was lifted. However, instead of everyone clearing out of Kate's, they all decided to hang around and celebrate the fact they were alive which meant more hours on the clock for me. Luckily the Charons were leaving in the morning so the boozing wrapped up a little while ago. After I clean up all this broken glass, I'm out of here. I don't care if Jesus Christ himself walks through the door and asks for a shot of bourbon. He can use his powers to pour his own drink.

"Need a hand?"

At the sound of the deep southern drawl, my body instantly locks and my gaze shoots to the man hovering over me. Bash's blue eyes pierce through me and the exhaustion I felt only seconds ago suddenly flees me. I open my mouth to reply but nothing comes out as he drops to his knees in front of me. His eyes leave mine as he makes quick work of picking up pieces of broken glass and I study his features, taking in his angular jaw that's covered in a days growth of scruff and the slightly crooked nose. The more my gaze wanders, the more intrigued I become. He has a full sleeve on his left arm, and I wonder if it curls around his shoulder, if the ink travels towards his chest or maybe down his back. I bet he has an incredible back full of taught muscles that leads to an even more incredible ass.

The thought shocks me and I immediately tell myself to take a step back and put some distance between us. But I'm paralyzed by him and the realization is unsettling.

Lydia, cut it out.

Knowing I'm close to undressing him with my eyes, I shake my head and finally will my feet to move. I blame my newfound attraction to the quiet Texan on exhaustion and rack my brain for something to say but the first thing that pops into my head is boxers or briefs. Note to self: don't engage in conversation with a man while tired.

"Shouldn't you be sleeping?" I stammer, silently praying he doesn't want another drink. My eyes drift to the top of his head, focusing on the fitted black baseball cap. He hasn't taken the damn thing off since he's arrived only sparking my curiosity more. Judging by the lack of sideburns I think it's safe to say he's not keeping much hidden under there.

Other than my husband, I've only been with two other men. None of them have been bald. If you're not threading your fingers through their hair while they're fucking you, what do you do with your hands? Clutching the sheets is for romance novels. I need something to hold on to. He's got nice shoulders. I suppose they'll do.

"Thank you," he quips, lifting his head slightly. Startled by the sound of his voice, I watch as his hands still. His eyes find mine under the rim of his hat and there is a glint of humor in a sea of blue.

"For what?" I ask confused.

"You said I have nice shoulders."

Fuck, Lydia, you're a mess.

There's no use in denying it so I shrug my shoulders in response. I mean, he does have nice shoulders.

Oh my God! Time to go.

"Do you have a dustpan or something to get these little pieces?"

"You don't have to do it," I say, finally coming to my senses. "You helped me out enough tonight," I add, recalling how he jumped behind the bar earlier to help me man the hooligans. I tried to shoo him away, but he kept at it for a good while before he was called away to say goodbye to Scout. Apparently, the president of the Charon MC got himself booked on a separate flight back home. If we ever cross paths again, I'll be sure to thank him for leaving this fine specimen behind for me to ogle. At least now I know my libido isn't dead.

Scrambling to my feet, I grab the tiny broom and pan from under the bar. I guess I was too busy counting the minutes until I could leave and breaking glasses to notice Bash had returned. Dropping back to my knees in front of him, I move to sweep the rest of the mess but his hand closes over my wrist.

"I've got it," he says softly, prying my fingers from the dustpan and broom. "You look like you're about to drop."

"I'm fine," I argue, reaching for the broom again. He moves out of my reach and diverts his attention to the task at hand, pushing all the tiny pieces into a neat pile.

"I'm observant," he continues, sweeping every scrap of glass into the dustpan. "You've been running on empty for days, darlin'."

An objection sits on my tongue as he rises to his full height, shifting both the dustpan and broom into one hand as he extends his free one. Feeling defeated, I huff out a breath and slide my hand into his. The simple touch of his fingers against mine shakes me to my core and I try to recall the last time I didn't flinch at a man's touch.

Lifting my eyes to his, I draw in a deep breath as he continues to warm me with his gaze.

"It's always the quiet ones," I whisper as he helps me to my feet. Chuckling, he gives my hand a squeeze before releasing it and I watch him walk, appreciating his swagger. Again, I shake the ridiculous thoughts from my head as he drops the glass into the garbage. With a glance in my direction, he pulls a bottle from the shelf and sets it on the bar. Realizing he wants another drink I fight the scowl tugging at my lips.

"Last call was an hour ago," I remind him, watching as his lips quirk ever so slightly as he ignores my comment and pours two shots. With his index finger, he nudges one towards me.

"Not looking to have you serve me," he croons, letting his gaze travel the length of me. It's not the first time I've caught him checking me out. However, he wasn't as conspicuous about it when we were pouring drinks for both clubs and I was smart enough to ignore it. Now, my defenses have somehow been broken down, and it's just a matter of who is going to make the first move.

"Well?" he questions, inching the glass a fraction closer. "You going to let me take care of you or what?"

Keeping my eyes on him, I lift an eyebrow and take the glass.

You're not that same woman.

You can live without fear.

It's just a drink.

He's not him.

I swirl the whiskey around like the professional I pretend to be before taking a step closer. I might be exhausted but I'm coherent enough to recognize when a man wants me and maybe I deserve to indulge in the attention for just one night. To feel like a woman and not a victim. To remember what it's like to live in the moment and not in fear.

Swallowing, I lift my gaze to his.

He'll be gone in the morning.

I'll never have to see him again.

No risk.

He's perfect.

"Not sure if a shot will cut it, cowboy. But thanks for the offer," I say evenly or at least that's the tone I shoot for. If I've learned anything in the last two years, it's how to fake a bravado.

Lifting the glass to my lips, I down the shot. It slides smoothly down my throat, and I wipe the excess liquor from my mouth with the back of my hand as I set the empty glass on top of the bar. We stand there idly, our eyes wandering and our hands still. When he doesn't make a move, I wonder if I've misread his intentions. It's a strong possibility seeing how long it's been since I've entertained a man or the idea of sex. As the seconds tick by, I start to feel foolish. Vulnerable. Everything I swore I'd never feel again. The urge to flee engulfs me and I decide to leave the task of cleaning our empty shot glasses for tomorrow. I reach under the bar for my purse and quickly sling the strap over my shoulder. I divert my eyes back to the handsome man just passing through.

It would've been nice.

It would've been liberating.

"Have a safe flight."

Without saying a word, he closes the distance between us and my breath hitches at the proximity. He lifts a finger to my shoulder, gently wedging it under the strap of my purse and tugs it down my arm. I watch as he places it next to my empty shot glass and lifts his full one. Knocking the amber liquid back, he turns to me. I wait for him to say something else, but all he does is stare. My insecurities start to get the better of me, and I wonder what he sees when he looks at me. Does he notice all my flaws? All my imperfections? Am I just a body and a means to his release?

"The shot was just a warm-up, Lydia."

With a wink, he rounds the bar and strides for the front door. I watch as he slowly slides the deadbolt into place. I wait for the fear to suffocate me, but it never does.

Nervously, I divert my attention away from him and grab a rag. I pretend to wipe down the bar as I try to remember if my bra matches my panties. Not because I'll be punished if it doesn't but simply because it exudes femininity. I also try to recall the last time I shaved my legs.

Acting on the nervous energy pulsing through my veins as he slides up behind me, I lift the bottle he used to pour our shots and return it to its rightful place on the shelf. His hand touches my hip and I go completely still. My eyes close as I relish in his gentle touch. Every thought and all my worries drift away from me as his fingers trail over my skin. Soon, the air leaves my lungs as he turns me in his arms, guiding our joined hands to the back of his neck. My heart hammers with anticipation as our eyes lock and the tips of his fingers gently graze the inside of my arm.

"You sure are pretty, darlin."

He wasn't kidding about the shot being a warm-up.

For in a single night, a mere couple of hours, Bash lit my whole world on fire.

And the best part?

I let him.

‘Shifting Gears’ by Janine Infante Bosco releases 22 October 2019 and is the first book in the Satan's Knights Prospect Trilogy. It is a spin-off from Khloe Wren's Charon MC universe and can be read and enjoyed as a standalone.

Other Charon MC Books:

Book 1:
Inking Eagle

The sins of her father will be her undoing… unless a hero rides to her rescue.

As the 15th anniversary of the 9/11 attacks nears, Silk struggles to avoid all reminders of the day she was orphaned. She's working hard in her tattoo shop, Silky Ink, and working even harder to keep her eyes and her hands off her bodyguard, Eagle. She'd love to forget her sorrows in his strong arms.

But Eagle is a prospect in the Charon MC, and her uncle is the VP. As a Daughter of the Club, she's off limits to the former Marine. But not for long. As soon as he patches in, he intends to claim Silk for his old lady. He'll wear her ink, and she'll wear his patch.

Too late, they learn that Silk's father had dark secrets, ones that have lived beyond his grave. When demons from the past come for Silk, Eagle will need all the skills he learned in the Marines to get his woman back safe, and keep her that way.

Book 2:
Fighting Mac

She's no sleeping beauty, but then he's no prince - just a biker warrior to the rescue.

For the past three years Claire 'Zara' Flynn has been at the mercy of narcolepsy and cataplexy attacks. But after she witnesses a shooting by the ruthless Iron Hammers MC, her problems get a whole lot worse. She's now a marked woman, on the run for her life.

Former Marine Jacob 'Mac' Miller has a good life with the Charon MC. He works in the club gym and teaches self-defense classes - in the hopes of saving other women from the violent death his sister suffered. When the pretty new waitress at a local cafe catches his attention, he wants her in his bed. But there's a problem. She's clearly scared of all bikers. Wanting to help her, he talks her into coming to his class. Mac soon realizes he wants to keep her close in more ways than one. But can he, when his club's worst enemies come after her?

When Zara disappears, Mac and his brothers must go to war to get her back. Because this time, she wakes up in a terrible place... surrounded by other desperate women, and guarded by the Iron Hammers MC. Can her leather-clad prince ride to the rescue in time to save her from hell?

Book 3:
Chasing Taz

He lived his life one conquest at a time. She calculated her every move… until she met him.

Former Marine Donovan 'Taz' Lee might appear to be a carefree Aussie bloke living it up as a member of the Texan motorcycle club, Charon MC, but the truth is so much more complicated. With blood and tears haunting his past and threatening to destroy his future, Taz is completely unprepared for the woman of his dreams, when she comes in and knocks him on his ass. Literally.

Felicity "Flick" Vaughn joined the FBI to get answers behind her brother's dishonorable discharge and abandonment of his family. Knowing Taz was a part of her brother's final mission, she agrees to partner with him to go after a bigger club, The Satan's Cowboys MC.

However, nothing in life is ever simple and Flick is totally unprepared to have genuine feelings for the sexy

Aussie. When secrets are revealed and their worlds are busted wide open, will they be strong enough to still be standing when the dust settles?

Book 4:
Claiming Tiny

Some rules were meant to be broken.

After being raised in foster care, Ryan 'Tiny' Nelson has no plans to settle down. But that idea goes right out the window when Missy shows up at the clubhouse. One taste of the Charon MC's newest club whore and he's hooked.

Love is the last thing on Mercedes 'Missy' Soto's mind when she runs to the Charon MC for protection. But the first time Tiny wraps his arms around her, he captures her heart in the process.

When things start unravelling, Missy panics and runs. Will Tiny find her in time to give her a Christmas to remember, or will he lose her forever once her past catches up with her?

Book 5:
Saving Scout

Nothing worthwhile in life ever comes fast or easy.

Twenty five years after first meeting the Charon MC's president, Scout, Marie is still waiting for him to realize they're meant to be together. But instead, he comes to her asking she hire his ex. Frustrated with his continued rejection, she leaves town for the weekend to clear her head and maybe find a man who'll help her forget her infatuation.

When Scout first met Marie, she was way too young, and he hadn't been looking to settle down. Over the years, he'd never bothered to rethink his stance. When he learns Marie has fled town, he panics and realizes he needs to step up and claim what has always been his. Tracking her down, he approaches her at her hotel and he finally lets the sparks fly.

But before they can ride off into the sunset, trouble brews and Scout is taken by an enemy from their past that neither of them knew had been waiting for them. Can they overcome this latest hurdle to finally find their happily ever after? Or are they doomed to always be apart?

Book 6:
Tripping Nitro

***Sometimes the one that got away comes
Back… bringing trouble with her.***

It's really her. Former Navy SEAL and member of Charon MC, Nitro can't believe his eyes when he finds his high school girlfriend in a bar nineteen years after she disappeared, taking his heart with her.

Alone and running from a stalker since she was 16 years old, Cindy has avoided all contact with the opposite sex in order to keep her mysterious stalker appeased. Now, with Nitro by her side, he vows to keep both her body and heart protected, but can she risk believing him?

With the help of his Charon MC brothers, Nitro keeps Cindy guarded while he attempts to woo her back into his arms. But just when he manages to break through her walls, she vanishes again. Will Nitro be able to put together all the pieces of the puzzle in time to save his first and only true love?

Book 7:
Scout's Legacy

*There's nothing he won't do to keep those
he loves safe.*

It might have taken Charlie "Scout" Dalton, the president of the Charon MC, over twenty years to see what was right in front of him, but once he did, he didn't waste a moment tying her to him. Now happily married to the love of his life, Marie, they were expecting a baby and had adopted little Ariel. His life was coming up roses.

Once ready to give up on Scout, Marie was now living her dream. Married to the man she's loved forever and carrying his baby in her belly.

But nothing in life ever goes to plan, and the birth of their baby is no exception. An unknown enemy comes to Bridgewater and chaos ensues. In the aftermath, Scout finds his loyalty to everything he holds dear tested. Will he be able to find a way to both save his club and be there for his family?

Book 8:
Mac's Destiny

This next club run will change their lives forever.

One day after Jacob "Mac" Miller returns from New York, Scout sends him on another club run. He must go to L.A. and deal with a mob boss who has set his sights on the Charon MC. Sabella is a blast from Mac's past he'd have preferred to leave there, but once he gets word of what the man is now up to, he can't let it stand and willingly leads the charge to go deal with him. Once and for all.

Zara is not happy with the club. Her man just returned from a run up to New York and after only one night home, he's back on the road, leaving her alone with their 10 month old daughter again. It wouldn't be so bad if little Cleo wasn't ill and getting worse.

Circumstances beyond their control test both Mac and Zara as their lives get changed forever in the aftermath of this latest drama that hit the Charon MC.